Christmas in Kentbury

USA TODAY BESTSELLING AUTHOR
CLAUDIA BURGOA

Also By Claudia Burgoa

Be sure to sign up for my newsletter where you'll receive news about upcoming releases, sneak previous, and also FREE books from other bestselling authors.

Christmas in Kentbury is also available in Audio

The Baker's Creek Billionaire Brothers Series

Loved You Once

A Moment Like You

Defying Our Forever

Call You Mine

As We Are

Yours to Keep

Collide with Me

Paradise Bay Billionaire Brothers

My Favorite Night

Faking The Game

Can't Help Love

Decker Family Novels

Unexpected Everlasting:

Suddenly Broken

Suddenly Us

Somehow Everlasting:

Almost Strangers

Strangers in Love

Perfect Everlasting:

Who We Are

Who We Love

Us After You

Covert Affair Duet:

After The Vows

Love After Us

The Downfall of Us:

The End of Me

When Forever Finds Us

Requiem for Love:

Reminders of Her

The Symphony of Us

Impossibly Possible:

The Lies About Forever

The Truth About Love

Second Chance Sinners :

Pieces of Us

Somehow Finding Us

The Spearman Brothers

Maybe Later

Then He Happened

Once Upon a Holiday

Almost Perfect

Luna Harbor

Finally You

Perfectly You

Always You

Truly You

My One

My One Regret

My One Desire

The Everhart Brothers

All my books are interconnected standalone, except for the duets, but if you want a reading order, I have it here → Reading Order

Special Edition: Amanda Shepard

Edited by: Brandi, Zelenca, Sisters Get Lit.erary Author Services, Anna Casillan

Dear Reader,

I write highly emotional romances that include thought provoking subjects. If you would like to see a list of them, please check the link below with more information.

TW Website

Happy Reading,
Claudia

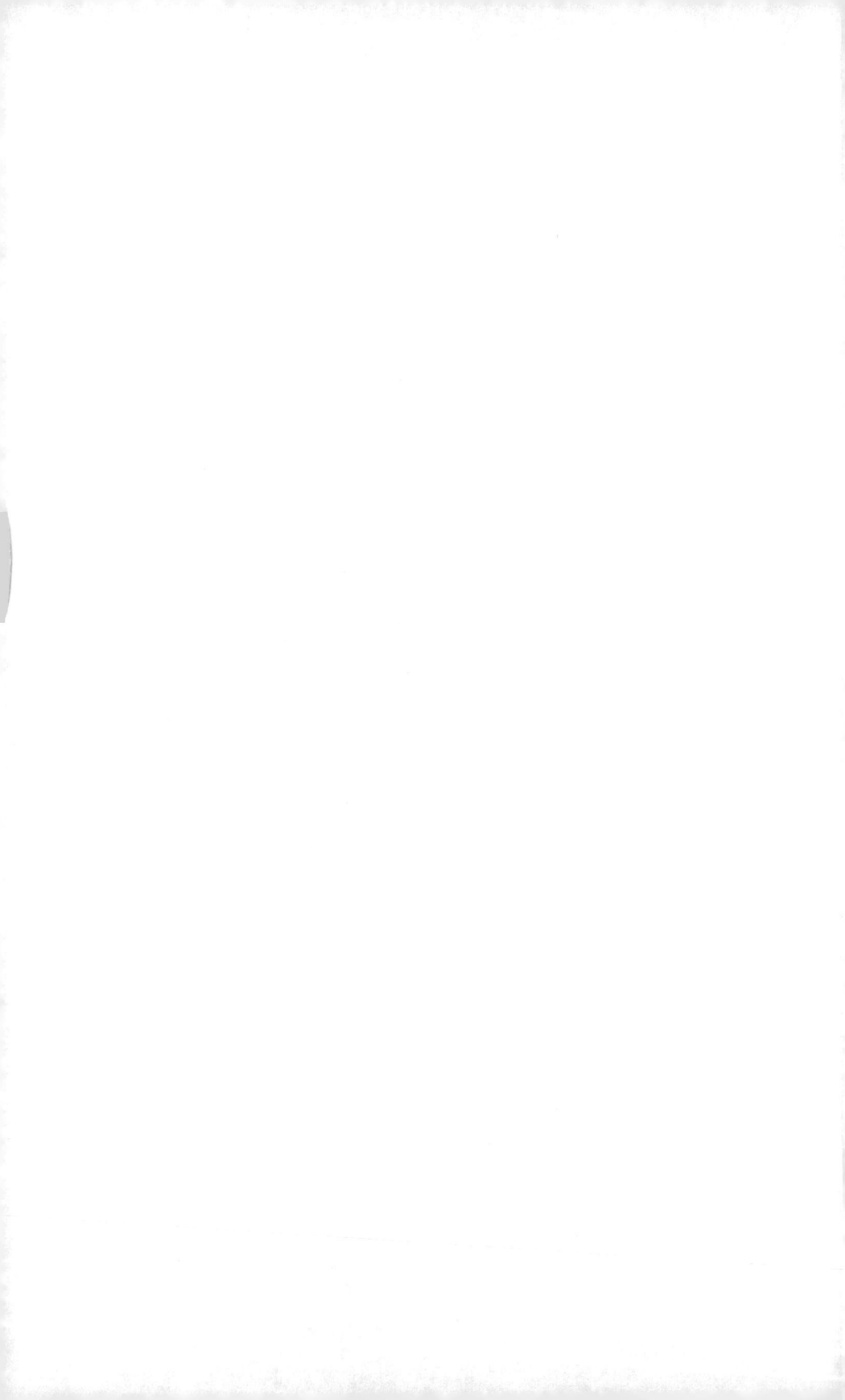

Prologue

Landon

I HATE surprises almost as much as I hate Sunday brunch with my parents. My family and I don't get along. It's a cliché, but we're like water and oil. I became everything they hate, and I hate everything they represent. My parents are judgmental. During my late teens and up until a few months ago, I fucked around—a lot— in every sense.

I went to MIT, but during my sophomore year I lost my scholarship. The dean called me irresponsible. My parents wrote me off as a failure, until I came back to Kentbury to take over my uncle's car repair shop after he died. I try to keep myself out of trouble and off the town's radar. I steer away from the women in town. But I do have fun with the tourists who stay at the lodge. It's simple. They're here for a week or a weekend. Then they're gone for good.

"Looks like I ran out of luck." I sigh and look down.

In the bouncy chair lies Cassie, my one-month-old baby. The fuzz of black hair is covered by a pink hat. Her arms aloft as if dreaming of cuddling her mother. I slide my pinky into her open hand and watch as her fingers curl around it. I feel her soft breath on the back of my hand. Already the tension is melting away as I watch my sweet little girl sleep in peace. She's so innocent, she doesn't know that our lives have been changed forever.

"Maybe I just got lucky," I whisper close to her ear. "You and I are going to make it work. I'll make you proud little one."

There's a light knock on the door.

"That must be Knightly coming to save the day," I whisper to Cassie and kiss her tiny hand before opening the door.

There's so much I could tell her about my best friend, but there's not enough time. I only tell Cassie what's important. "She's going to become your favorite person. We call her Lee for short."

When I swing the door open, I finally relax. Lee's here.

Her brown eyes narrow, locking her gaze on me. "I need a big explanation," she says handing me the shopping bags she carries with her.

"Hello, Lee," I greet her and stare at all the bags she brought as she unzips her blue parka.

"I got everything you asked for," she says. "Bishop is bringing the big items. What do you need them for?"

Her voice is neutral, but I know her well. She's easy to read. The expression on her face matches her mood. I know when she's excited about something. I can tell when she's tired or cranky. Or, like right now, when she's upset that I'm keeping her in the dark. As she takes off all her winter gear and sets her snow boots on the plastic tray, I close the door, avoiding the sight of her body.

I like to think of Lee Harris as my best friend. One of the boys. She's the kid I've been hanging out with since she could walk. I endlessly practice *not* noticing her sweet curves or the way her long, dark, curly hair cascades over her shoulders once she takes off her hat. I'm a shitty person and can't do relationships. I'd never do anything to jeopardize my relationship with Lee. Ever.

I tilt my head toward the living room. "Follow me."

Lee follows. "Oh my God, did Santa bring me a baby?" She claps once and takes out the tube of hand sanitizer that she always carries with her.

Without asking, she undoes the belt on the bouncy chair and takes Cassie into her arms.

"Hey, beautiful, welcome to Kentbury. You're going to love this place."

Cassie snuggles closer to Lee, who looks beautiful holding my baby. I swallow hard and remind myself that she's a friend who deserves a lot more than a guy who sucks at life.

"You're not going to ask anything?"

"The mom came to the lodge earlier, asking for you." She sweeps my body with her gaze. "Tall, dark hair, light blue eyes and was friends with the lodge's owner." Lee rolls her eyes and sighs.

"You and Damian need to stop sleeping around or…" Lee touches her mouth lightly with the tips of her fingers. "Oops, it happened."

"You could have warned me she was here." I grit my teeth.

"I could have." She shrugs. "Maybe next time."

I glare at her. She's not funny but I don't have the energy to deal with her banter. Though, maybe she doesn't have much energy either because she's not as witty as usual.

"How are you handling the news?" she asks with a serious tone though her gaze remains on Cassie.

"I'm dealing, I guess." I close my eyes briefly, taking a deep breath. "Can you picture me as a father?"

I gesture to myself, showing her the hot mess that I

am, then point to the apartment I live in, which is above the car shop.

"I'm a fucked-up guy who can't finish anything. I can't even get along with my parents. What am I supposed to do with a baby?"

"Love her," she answers. "You should give yourself some credit, Landon. She has the best dad in the world, and you two have me and my family."

I smile at her and say the obvious, "I can always count on you."

Lee studies Cassie. She smiles at her, but her face looks a little saddened. Her brown eyes are slightly red and watery. Was she crying? I'm sure it's nothing. Later, when I'm not busy with my baby, I'll ask her what's wrong. In the meantime, I have to learn how to be a dad.

Maybe I can find a book on how to be a father online. It worked with the car shop, and so far, I've managed it well enough.

Chapter One

Knightly

"DID SOMEONE CHECK-IN LAST NIGHT?" Marcy asks as we peer through the crack in the door, staring at the unconscious body splayed over the Egyptian cotton comforter.

I look at her with a questioning gaze. "No, this room should be empty."

"Well, tell it to that guy's ass," she says.

Some say *crisis* is my middle name. Actually, it's Rose. But if someone is in a crisis, I'm the go-to girl to solve most of the problems. I live in a small town where everyone knows… well, everyone. We don't lock our front doors, and that includes the main door of the Bed & Breakfast. For starters, it's a hotel so we have to keep the doors open. Also, no one trespasses in Kentbury.

"We should call the sheriff, or maybe your brothers," Marcy, the housekeeper, suggests.

Calling the authorities will start a rumor and before I know it, there'll be a crowd outside my business. I don't have time to deal with that aftermath. My brothers never show up when I need them, so I'm not going to bother with calling them either.

"Landon's on his way," I say, holding onto the wrench that I found in the garage on the way here with both hands.

When I fully open the door to the Royal room, I see the intruder, just like Marcy described him.

Clothes scattered carelessly around the room. Who is he? A serial killer, a stranded traveler, or just a drunk who decided to crash in my B&B to avoid an angry wife.

My shoulders tense, and I hold my breath. Maybe I should call the police. Terror surges through my body, but I relax when I feel a big hand squeezing my shoulder.

"It's okay," Landon, my best friend, whispers behind me.

"Is it?" I huff, upset at myself for having such an overactive imagination.

"You had a one-night stand, and you want me to kick him out?" His light blue eyes flicker with humor.

"Ah, he thinks he's funny." I groan as my eyes sweep over his tall, muscular figure.

People call me to solve their crises and I call him to solve mine—not the sheriff who happens to be my cousin or my brothers who never respond on time.

Landon Miller and I have known each other since before I could walk. Rumor has it that our mothers had been best friends since they were children. I wouldn't know, mine died shortly after I was born. He's my brother's best friend as well as mine. Though, sometimes, like right now, he can be a little obtuse. And if I don't stop him, he'll crack a few more jokes before he actually does something about the intruder.

"Hey, don't shoot me, Lee. I'm just trying to understand the big emergency," he says. "I take it he's not a guest. So, who is he?"

"We have no idea who he is. Marcy came to make sure the room is ready because we have guests coming in later today. She *found* him like that."

I scrunch my nose and stare at the bed. The guy is lying down on his stomach. His arms set above his dark brown hair.

Landon frowns, taking the wrench away from me. "How many times have I told you that these are tools, not weapons?"

I refuse to explain to him how the wrench could do

some serious damage. Landon always manages to make me edgy. As frustration boils in my belly, I focus on his industrial boots and hold my breath, trying to avoid his intoxicating scent. It's that woodsy aftershave he loves so much and traces of engine oil. It's so him. I wish I weren't so attracted to this man. Briefly squeezing my eyes shut, I gather all my strength to pretend he's not affecting me. That my gut isn't clenching because my ovaries are about to explode.

There's a saying that practice makes perfect. I keep practicing and yet, it gets harder to feign that I'm not in love with Landon Miller. Eighteen years of faking that I'm immune to the wide-set jaw, strong cheekbones, dark brows, and full lips can't go to waste.

Do I care about the way his white T-shirt stretches across his chest?

Nope. I don't care about his taut body.

I refuse to acknowledge any emotional or physical attraction to this man. Never mind that every time his light blue eyes focus on me, my heart flutters fast inside my chest.

"Hmm," he says, as he enters the room and I follow him with my eyes. "Bring a bucket filled with cold water and ice."

"Why would I do that?" I sneer. "It'll ruin the bed."

"Wouldn't you like to see Bishop cry like a little girl?" He pokes the guy with the wrench.

"Wake up, Harris." Landon's rough voice booms around the room. "Why are you here?"

"Ew, Hops?" I turn around, disgusted by the sight of my brother's naked body.

Perfect, just great. I just saw my brother's bare ass and if this is any indication, he must've been kicked out of his place.

"Five more minutes, babe," Bishop grumbles.

"Handle your friend," I say to Landon as I walk away. "I need this room, *now*. We have paying guests arriving soon."

"You owe me, Lee," Landon calls after me.

"I don't owe you *shit*," I mumble but I'm sure he doesn't hear me since I'm almost at the bottom of the stairs.

"You said a bad word," Cassie, who sits on the foyer couch, chides me.

"Clean those ears," I say playfully. "Your hearing is faulty."

"Ha, I heard you all right. You said *shit*," she repeats, giving me a mischievous smile so much like her father's.

"What have we told you? That's not a ladylike word, Cassandra," Landon reprimands his daughter.

"I just repeated what Lee said, Daddy," Cassie tattle-tales on me.

"I didn't know you brought her along." *Or I would have watched my fucking language.*

"It's Saturday and I can't stay at home *alone*." She

11

rolls her eyes. "I'm not old enough. He's going to have me do homework in his office while he works on a car."

"You can always hang out with me," I suggest.

"You're such a bad influence, I'm not sure that's a good idea," Landon jokes.

"She doesn't say shit much, only mouths *fuck* a lot," Cassie says.

I glare at her. "I thought we were friends."

"He says bad words too. You should make him put a hundred dollars in the swear jar every week," she accuses her dad, and I'm pretty sure she's having a blast with us.

"We need to talk." Landon's voice is a little more stern than usual.

I can't help but laugh when I realize he's biting back a smirk.

"Oh my," I say, clutching my necklace. "You're breaking up with me? I thought we had a good thing going between us. Was it my scones? I thought you loved maple scones."

"Do you have any?" He gives me a boyish smile.

"Nope, today we have cranberry scones. I can make you some coffee and you can tell dear Knightly what's bothering you."

"Can I have pancakes for breakfast, please?" Cassie requests.

"You haven't had breakfast?" I frown.

"It's barely eight o'clock, and you called with an *emergency*. Of course, she hasn't had breakfast yet."

Cassie points at her dad. "He promised you'd make pancakes for us."

"He did, huh?" I take her hand the same way I used to when she was a tumbling toddler. "You're going to help me, though," I say. "If we're lucky, Gramps might share some of his liquid gold with us."

Her light blue eyes widen, then crinkle with excitement. "Do you think we can make maple candy?"

"How about tomorrow?" I offer. "Today's a pretty busy day."

"How so?" Landon looks around the empty dining room.

"There's a bride-to-be coming to check out the place with her parents and her in-laws."

"Here? Not the lodge?"

"Ski resort," I correct him.

Last year, Damian, my oldest brother, decided to rebrand our businesses, and he started with the lodge. We now call it the Ski Resort at the Harris Estate. He also changed the furniture and renovated the entire building.

Damian wishes he could renovate the Victorian home where we run the B&B, but I won't let him. It's a historical building that's been in the Harris family for five generations. We own the land where the farm, the orchard, the gift shop, the house, and the lodge stand, and have since the late eighteen hundreds.

"This bride wants to find the perfect spot for the

wedding. A guest referred the B&B and the farm. Not that Dad will let that happen."

"The farm isn't a wedding destination," my father's voice booms through the kitchen before he even steps foot inside it. "That's what the lodge is for."

"Ski resort," I correct him, gritting my teeth.

"Mr. Harris." Landon nods.

"Grampa Harry," Cassie says as she runs to Dad.

"I didn't know my little girl was here." He hugs her and twirls her around the kitchen.

"Can we make maple candies?" she asks.

I glare at Landon for this one. She's just as stubborn as her father. They take the word no as a challenge. Their motto is *I'll make it happen.*

"Sorry, sweetheart, but we can't today. We have a full house, and we have to be scarce from the premises." Dad frowns, he's pretty upset at the possibility of offering new venues.

Financially, it means that we can book two or three events at once. If Damian buys the vineyard next door, the possibilities just continue growing. Dad doesn't see it that way.

"Can I come with you?" Cassie grins at him.

"I'll be at the *ski resort*," Dad says, proud that he said the right name this time. "If your father lets you, we can ski all morning. Then, I'll take you to the dining room for lunch and maybe some hot chocolate. We can spend the rest of the afternoon watching movies."

"And eating popcorn?" she suggests, planning her entire schedule for the weekend. I'm almost sure that later she's going to ask if she can stay at my house so tomorrow morning, she can go skiing again after brunch.

"If that's okay with you, sir," Landon agrees.

"She's always welcome to hang around with us. You guys are like part of the family, Landon," Dad mentions and looks at me. "What's for breakfast?"

They're not family, I want to clarify. Not because I don't want them to be, but because, well, they're just friends. This is the kind of situation that I hate, when I feel too comfortable with Cassie and Landon. I want them to be my family. My husband, my child, and my future. Sometimes it seems like I mean a lot more to Landon and other times he reminds me I'm just one of the guys.

Bishop has encouraged me to talk to Landon and find out where I stand. Damian insists that I should move on with my life. They're Landon's best friends and know him as well as I do. Maybe they're right. Either way, I know that Landon and I will never be a couple. I have to grow out of my teenage crush and find a way to fall out of love. If only I knew how.

I gLandon at Landon who is looking at his phone. His deep dimple shows as he smiles at whatever he's watching. Maybe he's scoring a date for tonight. My heart shrinks with disappointment. Yet, my pulse races as his light blue eyes find me. I melt when he winks.

"That new picture you added to your Instagram of you and Bob during your morning jog is cute."

I bite my lip, staring at his mouth, craving it, and wishing to know how he kisses. My gaze lowers to his sculpted chest and tattooed arms. He's dreamy. No wonder women flock to him like bees to flowers. I know one thing that they don't: Landon Miller doesn't do relationships.

Landon looks around the kitchen. "Where is the mutt?"

"Bob isn't a mutt, Daddy. He's a Newfoundland. It took us a long time to find him, remember?" Cassie corrects him.

They gifted him to me a couple of years ago for my thirtieth birthday.

"He's at the barn with the Alpacas," I respond.

"Lee, what are we having for breakfast?" Dad repeats.

"Cereal?"

"Pancakes," Cassie says, frowning at me. "We're making pancakes, scrambled eggs, and bacon," Cassie lists, sounding like she's already planning a big meal.

"Sounds like a treat," Dad says, smiling at me.

"It's not a holiday, people," I complain.

My family doesn't understand that this place has to be ready for the guests in a couple of hours. I'll have to bake several batches of chocolate chip cookies to replace the stench of bacon. Why don't they go to the resort for breakfast? I glare at them, but the anger subsides when Landon reaches out for my hand and squeezes it.

It's okay, he mouths.

"Come on, I'll help you," Landon offers, heading to the industrial refrigerator.

Chapter Two

Knightly

TRYING to erase the image of a nice family breakfast is impossible as I watch Landon stride toward his car. I stare at his broad, powerful shoulders. I find myself loving him and hating him all at once. Damn this idiot and his friendly gestures.

"Would you like me to make dinner for you tonight?" he asked after Cassie and Dad left for the barn.

Seriously? He should keep his offers and kindness away from me. It makes it hard for me to remember he's just a friend. Then why do I have the urge to grab my coat and step out into the freezing tundra and kiss him?

"Close your mouth and stop salivating for Landon Miller," Damian, my oldest brother orders.

"You're annoying," I complain. "Why are you even here? Didn't you hire an internationally recognized chef for the resort? You should have him cook for you."

Once breakfast was ready, he just waltzed into the house and sat at the table as if he had been invited.

"I'm just pointing out the obvious." He ignores my question. "Everyone knows you're in love with him."

"I. Am. Not."

"You should tell him," Bishop, who's been brooding all morning, says.

"Why would I do something that stupid?" I glare at my brothers who, for some godforsaken reason, are still hanging around. "Don't you have work to do?"

"Look, you're not fourteen anymore," Bishop explains. "Tell him how you feel, and if he doesn't feel the same, move on."

My throat is clogged, my legs are shaking. Is this an intervention? I don't have time for them *or* an intervention.

"Don't torture yourself like that," Damian says. "Just stop lusting after him."

I relax. It's just another day at the Harris house.

"But you have to stop playing house with him and his daughter. Don't get me wrong, I love Cassie like my niece but you... you love her as if she were yours." Damian just goes for the jugular and ends me. "She's not."

The sharp edge of his words stabs me right in my chest. I open my mouth to defend myself but it's useless. Even though his words shred my insides, he's right. I've known it all along. I just can't stop believing in miracles or loving them the way I do.

If I want to survive this day with my heart in one piece, I have to change the subject fast. Nothing says tag you're it better than *what's wrong with you, Bishop?*

"Are you cheating on Chloe?" I redirect the conversation toward Bishop.

"Why would you ask that?" Damian glares at Bishop, waiting for an answer.

"We found him butt naked in the Royal room," I say, grinning with satisfaction.

"Alone," he defends himself.

"You live a couple of miles from here," I argue. "So what? Did you drink too much, have a party, and after screwing someone else, you came here?"

Yes, I know I'm being evil, but with my brothers I have to be ahead of the game.

"Why did you come here?" I cross my arms.

He sighs, running a hand through his hair. "She kicked me out of the house."

"What did you do?" I ask, drumming my fingers against my opposite arm.

"Why do you always assume it was me? You don't even like her," he protests.

"That's not true."

"Please, Lee. You hate Chloe," Bishop insists.

"Hate is such a strong word. I just don't understand her. But that's not the point. What happened between you two?"

"She insists on leaving Kentbury."

"I'll give her a ride to the bus station," Damian, who really hates Chloe, offers.

"*We*. She wants *us* to leave," Bishop corrects.

Damian and I look at each other. *What the fuck?*

"Like on vacation, or she wants to move out of town?" I try to clarify this because she's not taking him away from his life.

Bishop loves tending to the farm. His life is the orchard, the cider mill, and the wholesale market. She can't just drag him away from here.

"Moving out of town." He tilts his chin toward the window. "But don't worry, I won't. My life is here."

I'm pretty confused. "Why would she propose to leave?"

"Well, she said that this isn't L.A."

"Did she *just* fucking realize that?" Damian, who thinks she's dumber than a sack of rocks, huffs.

"For fuck's sake, she's from Swanton, Vermont. Not Santa Barbara, California," I say, frustrated and sad that I'm right.

She's a gold digger who was just trying to catch the "rich guy." We're not rich. Actually, we have to work hard all year long to keep up with our expenses.

"It's over," he says with a shrug. "She wants me to choose her over my family and my life."

"Sorry about that." I step closer to him and squeeze his arm.

"It's okay. She's getting clingy and talked about marriage." He scrunches his face.

"She brought up the *M* word?" I gasp, faking horror. "How ridiculous of her. She should know better. You don't commit."

"Yep, I'm too young for that," he says ignoring my sarcastic tone.

"You're thirty-three," I remind him.

"As I said, too young," he repeats, nodding a couple of times.

Damian fake shivers and gives me a look that says, *he's right. I'm thirty-five and still not ready for commitment.*

What's in the water of Kentbury? Most men—including my brothers—can't say the word commitment without breaking out in hives.

"We will never agree on this subject." I sigh. "I'm staring at the calendar while I hear my biological clock ticking and you two swear you're not 'ready' for a commitment."

"What biological clock?" Damian frowns.

"The one that says I won't be able to have children when I hit a certain age," I respond.

Which, I'm not even sure when that is. The other day, I was reading an article about a fifty-year-old woman who gave birth—to twins. But what if, even at fifty, I can't find a guy to start a family with?

"Talk to Landon," Bishop insists, and we're back to the conversation I'm trying to avoid.

"And then what, make things awkward between us?" I ask with an annoyed voice. "I know he doesn't reciprocate my feelings."

How do I know that? I've been irrevocably in love with Landon Miller since I was fourteen.

"Maybe I should just go to a sperm bank and get inseminated," I mumble.

"Why would you do that?" Damian says. "You can't have a kid on your own."

"Because I want to have a family," I refute.

I can't even argue the point. It'd be stupid to tell him that Cassie's already eight and I miss having a baby around. I want a family with three or four children. I want a toddler I can chase around the house. I miss building snowmen the size of Cassie during winter. I want to have lots of stockings on the chimney and a special tree where I hang my kids' homemade ornaments.

Is it so bad to wish for what I can't have? Cassie used to love spending time with me. Now, she's searching for the next big adventure. The worst part is that Cassie's not even mine.

"What happened to the job offer?" Damian fires the question with a rough tone. He's in big brother mode and I hate they're focusing on me.

"It's just an interview. You need me here."

"We can hire someone to take care of the weddings and the B&B," Damian suggests.

I should remind him that we have a capable event planner. I choose not to.

"I'll find a manager for the gift shop," Bishop offers.

"I've never felt so... so... replaceable," I say.

The frustration and anger are gripping my throat. My stomach hardens, and I just want to go back to my house and hide under the bed.

"In less than five minutes you just told me one, that I'm expendable." I show him my index finger and begin to count. "Two, that no one could be in love with me, and three that I'm unfit to become a mother."

"Fuck, Lee, that's not what we meant," Damian growls.

"So would you like to clarify?"

"We're just saying that you seem restless. You deserve more than this town can offer. We're not a fancy hotel in the middle of one of the biggest cities in the world. Landon Miller doesn't deserve you. He's already settled down with his kid. If you want to have a kid, you'd be a great mom. Look at Cassie. You've done an amazing job with her, but she's not yours. You deserve better.

"A job you love, a man who adores you, a family with that man, that's what you deserve. Don't settle for the family business, the crumbs of love you get from the Millers, or a sperm bank. We want the best for you. I'd hire people to cover for you. Not because we don't need you. God knows this family needs you more than we need maple trees, snow, and apples."

I relax my shoulders. Okay, so they're concerned. They want what's best for me. Do they know what that is? I don't. Honestly, I have no idea if New York is better than Kentbury.

I was born and raised in this picturesque town. I went to college in Boston. It took me some time to get used to the big city. At first, the thick scent of smog and noise pollution blaring twenty-four-seven set me on edge. I missed the stillness and peace of my hometown during the summer and the white powder covering everything during the winter.

I prefer to walk in the small town where everyone knows each other. People stroll around the town square to go from the bank to the dry cleaners, the diner, or the movie theater. If we want a fancy dinner, we make a reservation at the ski resort. For a casual Friday, there's the pizza place down on Main Street.

I enjoy the aroma of winter when the air is cold and filled with moisture. In college, I got used to the fumes from belching vehicles. I could do it again. Moving to New York won't be bad, but I know in my heart that it'll never feel like home.

Yet, my brothers are right. The headhunter who contacted me is handing me an opportunity of a lifetime. Financially, professionally, and most of all, personally. I have to put some distance between Landon and me. If I'm lucky, I'll unfall in love—is that even a word? If it isn't, I just made it up. We'll call this next stage of my life, *operation unfall in love.*

"So, I just pack my things and go?" I ask.

"Why not? You can at least do it for a few years," Damian agrees. "Your experience might help the resort, even the gift shop."

"There're plenty of sperm banks in the city," I mention as an afterthought.

"Find a man, fall in love," Damian says.

"Because it's that easy." I roll my eyes.

"Not in this town," Bishop says. "Everyone knows you. They know you're in love with Landon."

"He knows?" I ask while my pulse spikes.

"I don't think so, but that's not the point," Bishop says, giving Damian an exasperated gaze.

Seriously? They're infuriating. Not only that, they're ganging up on me. I have work to do. They're stalling by giving me relationship advice. How ridiculous is that? Damian sleeps around with his guests—single or married, he doesn't discriminate. Bishop is a serial monogamist. He chooses women he knows won't stay long enough and once they leave, he's tossing someone new into his bed.

"I won't talk to him. If he ever finds out about my feelings, things will change between us, and I just can't lose Cassie."

I listen to myself, and God, I sound pathetic, desperate, and stupid. They're right, I have to make a plan, pack, and go. Kentbury might be my home. But if I don't leave, I'm going to die alone and unhappy. I feel a pang of sadness as I remember how happy I felt just a few minutes ago, back in the kitchen cooking for everyone, pretending that we were one big, happy family. My emotions storm inside my body. Somehow, between what my brothers just said and the moment I shared earlier, I become more aware of what's missing in my life.

The one thing I desire the most but would be missing from my life if I don't do something now. I text Landon, canceling tonight's dinner. I'll make a frozen pizza and watch Netflix with Bob.

It's time to move on.

Chapter Three

Landon

As I DRIVE to my shop, I try to delete the mental image of Lee while I was leaving the B&B. Her perfect curves molded by that tight sweater dress she was wearing. Her hazelnut hair tied into a messy bun. Her knee-high boots inviting me to do very naughty things to the only female friend I have. My wish for this Christmas is to be able to bend her over the kitchen counter, spread her legs—while she wears those boots—and eat her.

Stop, Miller.

This just-friends between Lee and I is more complicated as we grow older. Since Cassie arrived in my life, I haven't dated. Nor do I have any interest in being with a woman. Cassie became my life and Lee, my anchor. I only have time for my girls.

Who the fuck am I kidding? I don't want to look at anyone else, only at Lee. She's perfect. I just can't figure out how to make things work between us.

She deserves a lot more than a washed-out mechanic with a kid. Actually, the only good thing I have going for me *is* my kid. She's the best part of me. I'm happy the way my life is though. Do I miss having someone next to me? No, I've never had a relationship before. I can't miss what I've never had. Screwing up my relationship with Lee because I'm attracted to her isn't worth it. Not only would I lose a friend, but my daughter would also lose *her* Lee.

Knightly isn't her mom, but since Cassie came into my life, she's been very much like her mom. They have a special bond. My child might look like me, but she acts so much like Lee.

I just don't know how to get rid of all the emotions Lee provokes. Earlier, when I saw the naked intruder at the B&B, I wanted to kill him because I had visions of him being a one-night stand of hers who wouldn't leave; I can't stand the thought of anyone being with her.

I toyed with the idea of being the one guy who deserves her heart. I don't miss what I've never had, but

I yearn for what I *could* have with her. I want her in my arms, my bed, and my house. Every day I try to find time to be with her. At night, I wish I had the courage to kiss Lee, devour her mouth as I touch every inch of her body.

I just can't ruin our relationship. Maybe one day I'll be thankful for not fucking up our perfect friendship by acting on my desires. If only I knew how to have a romantic relationship. I park in front of my shop, taking a deep breath as I bury my emotions deep. I stay there for a long time, watching locals and tourists alike walk around the town square. The small ice rink that the local merchants set up every year is already crowded, and it's not even ten in the morning yet.

Cassie's too old to skate there. She claims the place is for babies and she's ready for the lake. I never thought I'd miss having a baby or a toddler in the house. It was so much fun to play with her.

I remember the day when she learned to skate. It was on the lake. Lee held her hands while I skated backward, telling her how to slide one foot in front of the other.

Damn, the image of Lee is back but this time the baby she holds is ours—a little boy. This is so fucking bad.

I pull myself together and get out of the truck and march toward the garage.

Jared's Car Repair Shop has belonged to my family for a couple of generations. It was my grandfather, Jared, who established it over sixty years ago. He loved cars and could spend hours tweaking an engine until it worked like new. I inherited his passion for fixing things. When I was young, I'd take apart the kitchen appliances just to see how they worked.

Mom tried her best to break that habit by grounding me and signing me up for every sport imaginable. Skiing, snowboarding, skating, ice hockey, field hockey during the summer, and even soccer. My brother Holden and I never won a medal, but if there had been some contest for who in Kentbury played the most competitive sports, we'd have won.

Needless to say, the times when I wasn't practicing, I was with my uncle at the shop. My parents didn't like it, but they were too busy with their own lives to stop me from visiting my uncle.

Unlike Grandpa Jared or Uncle Gerry, Dad hates the car shop, the engines, and the grease stains. According to my uncle, he couldn't wait to get out of town and become something better. Dad, however, never left. He's worked for the Main Street Bank for as long as I can remember. I, on the other hand, love to get under, or on top of, a car and spend hours tuning it.

My biggest passion is to take a beat-up old classic and restore it to its former glory.

Dad and I have nothing in common. My parents never understood Holden and me. The only time they were proud of me was when I got the acceptance letter to MIT and a full-ride scholarship. They hated me when I got kicked out of school.

I have work to do, and without Cassie, I can get more done. My heart stops when I enter the shop and see a message from Lee on my phone.

Lee: Thank you for offering to make me dinner, but I have plans.

Plans? I groan.

Landon: Do you need me to come by later?

Lee: No, I'm busy tonight.

That's bullshit. She told me she was free tonight, and if I wanted, I could leave Cassie with her. Though her dad offered to take my kid for the night. They made plans for tomorrow morning. I wish my parents were more like Steve Harris. He's always treated me like his son and loves Cassie like his granddaughter. Seeing that I was free in the evening, I thought it'd be a good idea to spend it with Lee. We could grab dinner, maybe go to the lake, and maybe a movie by the fire afterward.

But she doesn't have time anymore. *Fuck,* I swear under my breath.

That's not possible, something happened. I rehash the entire morning and our conversation after her dad left with Cassie. My stomach clenches when I figure out the answer—her brothers.

Bishop and Damian stayed behind to discuss an issue with her. That has to be it. They either pissed her off, or she has to help them with the resort or the farm. Maybe

Chloe is moving out of Bishop's and Lee has to be around. No, if that's the case, Bishop would be calling me to help with the move.

I have a niggling feeling that she's canceling because of them. I swear those two treat her like the oldest of the siblings instead of the baby of the family. They'd be lost without her—just like I would.

Landon: What can I do to help free up your time?

Lee: Nothing.

Nothing?

Is she blowing me off?

If she's upset with me, she'd tell me. She always does. So then why is she suddenly saying that she's busy? This is so unlike her. Lee's a pretty easygoing person. She's a fighter, one of those people who would make the impossible possible. Even if she had to put out a fire, she'd be free in the evening. She'd call me to help her with it.

Maybe that's the problem. She's always taking care of everyone. I try to keep an eye on her. Be the person she needs when she's falling and there's no one else around to catch her. With the holidays, there are a ton of emergencies that she has to handle. I try to be there for her and find ways to give her a break. I thought cooking for her would be nice. She beamed when I offered. There has to be a good reason why she suddenly canceled on me.

Landon: Busy how?

Lee: You wouldn't understand.

33

Landon: Why are you canceling on me?

Lee: Like I said, I have things to do. It's Saturday. I have a life you know.

I stare at the text, analyzing each word. What does having a life have to do with me cooking her dinner?

Did I piss her off?

I work hard to stay away from her bad side. That's a place where only her brothers belong. Not me. Instead of texting back, I call her, but I get her voicemail—three times.

Looking at the clock, I decide to start working and let her be for now. She's busy and I have a sweet 1963 Corvette waiting to be brought to life. Hopefully, the replacement parts I need will arrive today because there's a big storm coming next week. The delivery services won't drive to Kentbury until the roads are clear.

After I put on my work clothes, I try calling Lee one more time with no luck.

"What is happening with you, Knightly Rose Harris," I say out loud, staring at the phone.

I give up and send her one last text.

Landon: *I'm sorry if I upset you. Let me make it up to you.*

Chapter Four

Landon

THE HARRIS SKI RESORT's lobby is like a comfortable, homey living room of a cabin. It has a central gas fireplace ensconced in a tubular glass case, wall dividers made up of iron banisters laid together like earthen wrought iron gates and adorned with iron maple leaves. To the left, there's a floor-to-ceiling window where we can admire the slopes. It's fancier than it was a year ago, yet the architect who renovated the place made sure to keep the quaint, cozy feel of the establishment.

"What's going on, Miller?" Damian greets me.

"Where's Lee?"

"You can't find her at the B&B, her house, or with Dad?" he asks confused.

"Would you mind tracking down your sister, please?" I show him my phone. "I've been trying all day, and she's been ignoring my messages and sending me to voicemail."

"Lee?" He furrows his brow. "If you're looking for Cassie, she's already at Dad's. They left after having an early dinner. André prepared some snacks for them to take home."

Cassie has André, the lodge's chef, wrapped around her little finger just like everyone else. We hired him a year ago to make the restaurant one of the best in the area, not to cater to my child.

"No, I'm looking for Lee," I speak slowly, trying to bring back his attention since he's already staring at the front desk.

"What, Lee?" he asks without even looking at me.

Great, I lost the fucker.

"Yes, she's five foot three, hazelnut color hair, dark eyes, and looks somehow like you—but pretty. She goes by the name of Knightly. We call her Lee, and she usually wants to kill *you* because you upset her."

He focuses his attention back on me. "Miller, I love my sister, but I don't keep track of her. Since you're free, why don't we go to the restaurant?" He invites me like he used to do when we were twenty-five. It was back when he started working at the lodge, and I had come back from Boston to take over the shop.

"I saw a group of guests that might do it for tonight."

"You're not twenty anymore, Damian," I say quietly since there are guests around.

He chuckles. "Should I settle down, Miller?"

"No, but at least don't be fucking around with your guests. It was fun ten years ago. But you're thirty-five."

"Should I start behaving like you?" He stares at my hands. "I don't see you settling down. If you're warning me because you think I might knock up a girl, *I use condoms.*"

"I did too, and fucker, they don't always work," I say. "Think about the reputation of the resort. Why would I want to stay at the place where the owner might or might not fuck my wife or girlfriend?"

He takes a step back as if I just punched him in the face. Somewhere along the way, Damien lost perception of what matters. He lives in his own reality where he keeps the business afloat and tries to make it the best. Sometimes it feels like he lost his humanity.

"I get it, keeping the family business going is important. Finding an outlet helps you baLandon your life. But be *careful* with what you're doing. Did Lee know that you were planning to sell her B&B?"

"That was a couple of years ago, and I didn't do it," he growls.

"Because I stopped you," I remind him. "Until you pay me back, I own half of this place. Do your siblings know that?"

His eyes widen. Of course they don't know shit. He likes to know everything that's happening with the farm and the B&B but never tells them what's going on with the resort.

"Now, find your sister. She'll answer your call."

He huffs but sends a text. We don't speak as we wait for her response.

Where are you, Knightly Rose?

"She's at the creamery getting ice cream before heading home."

"What the fuck?" I glare at him. "She's doing exactly what I told her we should do earlier today. Why would she cancel on me?"

"Maybe she had things to do, and she finished early. Who cares?"

I do, fucker. I glare at him. We've never talked about Lee and I becoming something else, but I guess there's a mutual understanding that I can't break the bro-code. What would he do if I did?

"I'm going to the restaurant. I'll have André make something for her. Maybe ask for some chocolate cake to go with her custard."

"Why would you do that?"

He might have graduated from fucking Harvard, but his skull is too thick to comprehend human behavior and emotions.

"Because that's what you do for the people you care about. You do things that will cheer them up," I respond, exasperated.

"You care about Lee?" he asks, confused.

I flip him the finger and leave. There's no use explaining to an emotionally constipated man how relationships work.

Not that I'm in a relationship.

Chapter Five

Knightly

TODAY WAS one of the busiest days of the year. I'm spent, but also satisfied with the results. After the crazy morning with my family, I had plenty of time to make sure that the B&B felt like a home away from home for the guests. I was also able to package the chocolate chip cookies and set them in the gift shop for sale. Booking the weekend for the bridal party was risky, but worth it. Gloria, the bride-to-be, loved Kentbury, the B&B, and the resort.

Gloria found a few places where her wedding could be spectacular. Thankfully, Bethany, the event coordinator, convinced her to keep the ceremony and celebration within the resort. We can't predict the weather, and during the winter it's always cold. She'd have to wear a coat over her beautiful gown.

She's booking the B&B for her and her bridesmaids. She'll then move to the honeymoon suite at the resort for the wedding night, leaving her bridal party at the B&B.

Bethany is a genius. It's such a shame that my brother can't understand that we have a diamond on our staff. A diamond who I think has the hots for our chef André. Not that I should be nosing around their business, I'm just envious of them. It's Saturday, and I don't have anything nor *anyone* to do tonight. Unless my vibrators count.

That sounds terrible, but I'd give anything to have sex with a man and not one of my sex toys while I think of Landon Miller and his big, calloused hands making me come.

Resigned to spend my night alone with a pizza and Netflix, I drive home. However, I take a detour toward downtown and park right by the creamery. I might not have a date, but I can have a pity party loaded with carbs. Life is better with vanilla custard mixed with fresh berries, and I have plenty of berries at home. I wish I had thought about this before I left the resort. André's chocolate fudge cake goes perfectly with it.

Ugh, why didn't I fall in love with him? I'd be having hot sex tonight, and he'd feed me all my favorite foods.

I take a deep breath and decide to buy a half gallon of custard so I can save some for tomorrow. I'll have to run an extra mile for the next week or two, but who cares? I'll feast on chocolate cake and custard tomorrow.

As I'm about to throw my phone inside my purse, I notice a text from Damian.

Damian: *Where are you?*

He's not one to care about my whereabouts. He only cares when he needs me. I answer and then ask *why?* While I wait for his response, I stare at the small ice rink in the middle of the town square. My parents and some of the business owners around the area began the tradition. It attracts tourists. This place and the season remind me so much of Cassie when she was just a baby and we brought her to take her first picture with Santa.

The nostalgia is killing me tonight.

When I enter the creamery, the bell above the glass door rings. The place is busy with tourists. I'm glad I don't have to deal with people asking me where Cassie or Landon are.

"Where's Cassie?" Mrs. Bowman, the owner of the creamery, asks.

I swallow the grunt and smile at her.

"I made hot cocoa flavor today," she says. "I was hoping you'd bring her since it's Saturday and the ice rink is open."

"She's with my dad tonight," I answer, sighing.

"I'm glad. You and Landon need some alone time. Do you want to take a pint home for tomorrow?"

Mute, I stare at Mrs. Bowman. There're so many things I should tell her. Like Landon and I don't need time alone. That we don't share a home. We're not a couple. I don't though, because what if she says *I know, but you're in love with him.*

Does everyone see me as the pathetic loser in love with her best friend?

I don't say anything. Even though I want to leave, I order a pint of hot chocolate, and a pint of marshmallow rainbow because it's brand-new and we always try the new flavors together. I get half a gallon of vanilla custard, and because I just can't help myself, I also order a pint of peppermint ice cream for Landon because I'm a sucker for that man.

God, I need another intervention. A *real* intervention, not a talk with my brothers while they try to tell me what to do.

"Say hi to Cassie and Landon from me," Mrs. Bowman says when she hands over the bag with the ice cream.

"Sure, Mrs. Bowman." I fake a smile, realizing that she really thinks I'm an extension of them.

We're not a happy family.

"Tell Landon that I added the box of chocolate

peppermint baskets he ordered. Do you think he'd like to try the marshmallow sprinkles?"

What are marshmallow sprinkles?

She doesn't wait for my response and leaves me standing in front of the register.

"Here." She hands me a tub of tiny snowflake shaped marshmallows.

I frown. Where does she get these novelties?

"How much do I owe you?"

She waves her hand and shakes her head. "It's on the house. Landon never charges me when I need an oil change. He always helps me when my car, the appliances, or my furnace, break down."

That's awfully nice of him. He's always looking after everyone, and sometimes he doesn't charge. I wish everyone could be more like him.

"Thank you," I say because the second option is to pull out my wallet and explain to her that we're not together.

Mooching off my best friend's favors isn't very neighborly of me. I'm usually verbal, but today I've been stopping myself from clarifying my relationship with Landon too many times. Earlier while I was talking to Bethany, she asked me if I was going to get married at the farm when Landon and I finally decided to take that step.

We're not together.

"Drive safe, dear," she says, waving at me. "The roads are starting to get icy. I'll call Landon to let him know that you're on your way home and to look out for you."

I press my lips and nod. If I get the job in New York, I'm going to make sure everyone knows that Landon and I aren't an item. If not, they might start a rumor that I abandoned him and his daughter.

Chapter Six

Knightly

IT TAKES TWICE the time it normally does to get home. There's black ice on most of the intersections, and some drivers are skidding as they abruptly brake when they come to a stop sign or a red light.

Once I turn onto my street, I relax a little. No more cars driving around me as if they were at the Daytona 500.

This isn't sunny Florida, it's freezing Vermont.

I open the garage door, drive the car inside, and I spot *him* leaning against the doorframe of the entrance. He's wearing a gray Henley shirt, the sleeves already rolled over his tattooed, corded arms.

"Hi," I greet him, getting out of the car with the small pizza box and bag of ice cream.

"The roads are terrible," he says, taking me into his arms and giving me a hug. "You should've called me to come get you."

"I can drive on icy roads."

"It's not about you, but the other drivers." He takes the shopping bag from me. "You went to the creamery to stock up for the winter?"

"Nah, I just bought a few flavors that might not be there tomorrow." I sigh and unzip my jacket. "Why are you here?" I ask, which is better than *don't you understand that I can't hang out with you anymore?*

"You've been dodging my calls and messages all day long. I thought it'd be best to check on what's going on with you. Since it was too cold to wait outside, I let myself in. I hope that's not a problem."

"It's not. That's why you have a key."

I shed my coat, take off my snow boots, and stare at the dining room table. "I have pizza."

"You only bought a personal-sized pizza," he says.

"How do you know that?"

"It's Kentbury. We have a pretty good communication system in place—it's better than Twitter." He winks. "Almost as effective as Instagram or text messages. Mrs. Bowman called to alert me that you were driving back home. She chided me for letting you drive on the ice."

I sneer. "I. Can. Drive."

"That's not the point. She told me that you had gone to buy pizza right after—but a small one."

"Is that why you brought dinner?"

"No, I already had it—and she knew that too." He chuckles. "She thinks I'm a pretty thoughtful guy."

"How does she know that you had dinner?" I groan. This wouldn't be happening in New York.

"It's Kentbury," he repeats, which must be the reason why everyone in town knows that there's a big dinner on my table—for the two of us.

"Let's sit down, the food is getting cold."

"I canceled," I mumble, staring at my table.

"Lee, what did I do?" he asks, frustration dripping from every word.

"Nothing," I say dryly, keeping myself strong because my heart is melting at the sight of the fancy dinner that he brought.

Everything that I love from André's cuisine is here. Smoked salmon, potato cakes with herbed crème fraîche, shrimp pasta, and cucumber farro salad. There's a bottle of wine and glasses, and he set up the table. With a couple of candles, this would be considered a romantic dinner. This is the part of the night when my heart beats fast with hope.

In a couple of hours, when Landon reminds me that I'm just one of the guys, it'll be teary, broken, and hurt. Like me, my heart just doesn't get it. This is precisely why I'm in a rut. Landon does something sweet, I fall in love a little more, and then he stomps on all of my dreams.

"I pissed you off. Just tell me what I did so I can fix it."

"Why would you assume that?"

"I know you," he says quietly.

"You do?" I ask skeptically, laughing on the inside.

Buddy, you don't know shit.

"What's with you Harrises? Of course, I do. I've known you guys since we were kids."

I guess there's that. He knows me as well as he does my brothers. I'm just one of the guys. A part of the bunch. His bud.

"Let me put this in the freezer and wash my hands," he says. "Where's Bob?"

"At Dad's, Cassie convinced Dad to take him with them. She needs a pet," I say casually. Hopefully, he'll get her a dog this Christmas.

She's been begging for one since she was six. I'd buy her one, but Landon insists they're not ready for a dog. He should start by buying a house and moving out of the apartment above his garage.

"You bought a lot of ice cream. I hope you're going to share some of the peppermint ice cream with me."

"It's yours, she just assumed." I shrug and stop myself from saying that the entire town assumes we're together and maybe he should do something to clarify our situation. Because even I believe it sometimes.

"By the way, she didn't charge me." I bring up the free ice cream before he thanks me for buying it. "She mentioned something about her oil changes."

"Sometimes I take care of her car or the appliances around the creamery," he says casually, as if it's not a big deal.

"You're a good guy."

He shrugs. "I just help out my neighbors."

He pulls out the chair for me. Once I take a seat, he sets a napkin on my lap.

"Next time, I promise to cook."

"Cassie's with my dad, you could go to the resort and find yourself a hot date," I suggest as he pours the wine.

"I prefer to be here, *with you.*" His low voice resonates inside my chest, and my heart flutters.

Oh, how I wish that were true, and he wanted to be with *me.* Not with his friend Lee.

"Are you going to tell me what happened?" he asks.

He's seriously not letting it go, is he?

"It's been a busy day. Bishop, Damian, and I were discussing the business."

"Is everything okay?" He narrows his gaze. "Is he planning on selling any acres or a part of the farm?"

"No." I choke on the wine. "He wouldn't dare. Do you know he's toying with the possibility of buying the vineyard next door?"

"That'd be an interesting acquisition." He nods a couple of times. "Holden would entertain the idea."

Landon's lost in thought while we eat. After a couple of minutes, he shakes his head and says, "Sorry, I shouldn't be thinking about the vineyard. I'll worry about it some other day."

"That sounds so unlike you, anything you'd like to share?"

"Not really," he says, brushing away the conversation. "Why don't you tell me what happened today? I saw a large group at the B&B when I went by."

We talk about my day and the guests who I spent most of the day with. I tell him all about Gloria, how laid back she is, unlike her mother and future mother-in-law. They came with her, along with her sisters and the bridesmaids. The groom was awesome. He participated, and yet, he stayed out of the way. When the mothers became overwhelming, he stopped them politely. I liked the couple. I'm sure they'll make it in the long run.

"It's going to be a great wedding," I continue, excited by the prospect. "They signed the contract and gave us the initial deposit." I explain how Bethany's going to set the venue and how the B&B is going to play into the equation.

We have the B&B booked, and they reserved twenty rooms at the resort. They might block out more rooms as the RSVPs start arriving next July.

"Bethany's a great asset," he agrees with me. "We just need to keep her away from Damian."

"Oh, I don't think Damian would make a move on her," I assure him.

"He wouldn't, but he likes to micromanage everyone," he explains. "Bethany hates it."

I lean forward and look around before I whisper, "I think Bethany and André are an item."

He smiles and rolls his eyes.

"What?"

"Leave them alone, okay?"

"You knew! I can't believe you didn't tell me," I say, glaring at him.

"What have I told you about gossiping?"

"It's not gossiping. It's keeping each other informed about the ongoing events in our precious town."

He rolls his eyes.

"I caught them a couple of weeks ago," he confesses. "Why do you think André didn't protest about this dinner? He wasn't happy about the combination of dishes. He said they clashed and I'm pretty sure he said fuck you a few times in French. Still, I'll use this information to make sure you get your favorites."

He winks at me, and I can't help but sigh.

Then, when he thinks I'm relaxed enough, he throws out the question, "Are you going to tell me what's going on?"

His concerned voice and those light blue eyes filled with fear convince me to say at least something to him.

"My brothers persuaded me to go to New York City."

"Are you taking a vacation during the busiest season?"

His gaze focuses on me, holding it. Then, his eyes widen as he realizes what's in New York City.

"You said you weren't interested in that job." He doesn't even let me respond before he continues talking, annoyance clear in his tone. "Why would you move? The B&B is here. *It's yours.* You love working there. This town is your life, you love it."

It is mine. A year ago, Dad signed over the deed to me. The profits remain in the family, just like everything we own. However, the Victorian house is mine.

"There's nothing wrong with trying new things." I explain at least part of why I'm considering leaving.

Bishop would tell me this is the right time to start the conversation. Confess my feelings, so Landon can let me down gently and I can move on.

I'm not ready to do something like that. Most likely our exchange would look like this:

"Landon, I'm in love with you."

He'll choke on his own saliva and spit out a couple of words like "Excuse me?"

He's going to look like a blindsided deer and would either run away or he'd feign ignorance. I'd clarify, "I have feelings for you."

With all the patience in the world and the sweetest voice he'd say, "Lee, I care about you too. You're like a sister, well, more like a brother."

"But I love you," I'd insist.

"That's cute, thank you," he'd finish and just go away.

Either that or he might just tell me, *"Are you serious, Lee? I mean, look at you. We're just friends, there's no way I can take you seriously."*

Whichever way, his words will shred my heart into pieces which he'll toss into a bonfire. I'll watch as they become ashes that the wind blows away. I'll never find them, and of course, I'll never be able to put myself back together.

My way is so much easier: moving on, swallowing my feelings, and learning to live without him.

"This is your home," he insists. I glare at him, hurt. "Sorry, I just don't get it." He runs a hand through his hair and starts picking up the dirty dishes.

"Every time you do something, I'm there to support you. I'd expect the same coming from you," I say bitterly.

"Are you saying that I don't support you?" He's not raising his voice, but he sounds disappointed. "Usually, I don't give a fuck about what people say or don't say. I couldn't care less about what they think of me, but you." He huffs. "You, I care about. I give a shit about what you think or how you perceive me. I can't believe you doubt me."

"Hey, I'm not doubting you. But right now, I would love for you to say something like, Lee, go get the job. You'll kick ass in New York."

Landon presses his lips together. His gaze focuses on the empty bottle of wine. "I thought this town was enough for you. I guess you want more out of life. If that's what you want, then I'll support you."

"Please, don't smother me with your excitement."

"What do you want from me, Lee?" His eyes find mine. "It's like there's something you're upset about, but you won't tell me. I did something to you that has upset you to the core. You can barely look at me. I can't fix anything if you won't tell me what's bothering you."

"There are things that you can't put back together or solve."

"I can always try," he insists.

"Kentbury doesn't have everything I need. Look at me. I'm thirty-two, single, and alone."

He grunts. "You're not alone. You have your dad, your brothers, Cassie, and *me*."

"Yeah, but it'd be nice to have a boyfriend, a partner. Maybe even a husband. When I was giving a tour earlier today, I was thinking to myself *I want that*."

"A wedding?"

"A man who sees me like there's no one else in the world but me. He knew what she needed even before she spoke. It's about the stolen caresses, the conversations they had without words. She was telling him that in a couple of years, they'd bring their kids to see where they got married."

"You want children."

"My time is running out. I run a successful business, but success isn't everything." I tap my wrist. "I want kids, a husband, and my own family. I love Dad and my brothers, Kentbury, and my B&B. But I want to love someone." I pause and look at him briefly because I do love someone, it's just unrequited love. "I want a man who loves me back."

"We love you, Lee."

I sigh. "Dad might be single, but he has us. You have Cassie. If you look closely, I don't have anyone. New York might open up the possibilities."

He looks at me for a long time and nods. "I get it. There's nothing here for you."

"I know." I swallow the tears and go to the sink to wash the dishes.

He couldn't have said it better: I'm not interested in being a part of your happiness.

"The interview is Tuesday," I say as I set the silverware in the dishwasher. "My brothers said they have everything covered."

"Have you bought a plane ticket?"

"No, I'm driving."

"You can't drive while there's a storm hitting the East Coast," he warns me.

"Are you going to complain about my driving skills? I think I'm a good driver, Landon," I say, biting back the words, *fuck you, I drove during a blizzard to take your child to the hospital when she had a high fever and you were stranded in Burlington.*

I don't say a word.

"You are, but it's not safe. Take the train or a plane tomorrow night, I'll pay for it if you need it."

"I can't leave tomorrow. I'll leave on Monday and still have plenty of time," I protest.

"And you say that Cassie's stubborn because of me," he says, annoyed. "She got that from you."

I turn off the faucet and turn to look at him. "See, there's another positive thing about me leaving. I won't be a bad influence on your kid."

"She looks up to you, Lee. I don't want to play the Cassie card, but have you thought what you leaving will do to her?"

His words punch me in the gut. Have I thought about what this will do to Cassie? Has he ever thought about what Cassie's done to me? Please, don't get me wrong, I've adored that child since the first time I held her in my arms. But before that, I cried for three straight hours while I bought everything she needed.

He had a baby with another woman.

I would remain Lee forever.

I'm still just fucking Lee.

"She'll be fine. I'm just Lee, the family friend. I babysit her when you need me to. My dad will be happy to take on the role."

He shakes his head. "You're more than *just Lee* to Cassie and me."

"What do you want me to do, Landon? Stay because of Cassie? I'll be fifty, alone, and the only picture with a kid that I'll have over my fireplace will be the picture of my friend's kid who sends me a Christmas card if she remembers."

It's a miracle that I'm holding it together. I love that little girl as if she were mine. She's never going to be more than Cassie. At least she calls my brothers uncles. To her, I'm Lee. I'll never be Mom.

"I…" He runs a hand through his hair and lets out a breath. "You're right. Let me know if you need anything while you're away."

"You're leaving?"

"It's getting late, and the roads are bad. The tow truck company might get busier than usual. If that's the case, the guys will need me."

"Okay."

When he gets to the door, he stops and lowers his head. "I wish I could offer you what you need, because I hate losing you."

Once he's gone, the tears begin to fall one after

another. My heart is breaking because his words just solidify what I've known all along. He's never going to feel the way I do. For hours, I stare at the closed door, wishing that he'd have stayed and given me at least a kiss before we said goodbye.

Chapter Seven

Landon

WHILE LEE DESCRIBED HER FUTURE, I felt a familiar jolt of dismay. I'm so used to being told that I'm just a mechanic who can't offer more to the one child I accidentally had. Not that I consider Cassie an accident. She's my lucky charm. So far, I've done well enough for her, but I couldn't be everything that Knightly Rose wants.

A husband who'd cater to everything she needs. Someone who can give her what she deserves. Nothing I do will compare to a college degree and a job at a fancy office in the middle of Manhattan. She dated a guy like that when she was in college. Mark, Zack, or was it Sam? I can't remember his name, but she seemed happy with him. They broke up when she decided to move back to Kentbury.

Once she settles in New York, she'll find someone like him. Definitely, not me. I wish I had told her how much I need her. That maybe my kid isn't hers, but Cassie loves her so much—like a mother. I hate to accept that my mother's right about me. At least I have my Cassie.

When I get home, I go into the garage. Carson, one of the guys who has worked for us since my uncle owned the place sits by the desk in front of the old switchboard.

"Why are you here, boss?"

"In case you guys need me," I answer as I put on my work clothes.

I might as well get something done tonight.

"It's too cold, shouldn't you be at home with Lee? You brought her a fancy dinner." He takes out his phone. "At your age, I'd rather be at my house with my woman."

"Go home to your wife, I'll take care of everything," I say.

"You should be at home with Miss Lee. Why bring her a fancy dinner if you're going to leave early? You kids don't know how to woo a woman."

Carson's a big help around the garage, but annoying when it comes to my personal life.

"I don't understand why you're not staking your claim. She's pretty, smart, and sweet. Just like her mama. Everyone was in love with Rosie." Carson composes himself. "Well, not me. I love my Diane."

"Lee needs a guy from the city. Someone who will give her what she deserves. I'm just a mechanic."

He laughs. "You sound just like your mama when she broke Gerry's heart."

I stop in my tracks and turn to look at him. "What did you just say?" I narrow my gaze at him.

"Gerry and your mom dated when she moved here from Connecticut with her father. They were together for a year or two, but since he chose to stay in Kentbury to take over the business, she moved on with your dad."

"My mom and Uncle Gerry?" I repeat, astonished.

"Well, I shouldn't be telling you this, but you seem to be thinking less about yourself. You're a good man, Landon. Look at what you've done with the place. Your grandfather would be proud of you, and so would Gerry. He knew you'd save it and make it better."

My uncle was fun. I learned a lot from him. To fix cars, to look after my friends, and to never give up. When I lost my scholarship, he offered to pay for school if that's what I really wanted, but he doubted I did. He was right. I was just doing everything for my parents.

"He taught me everything I know," I say, looking around the garage.

Most of his posters were gone, along with the old equipment. I renovated the entire place and made sure my guys were trained to deal with all kinds of cars and technology.

"He taught you how to fix a car. You learned how to run the business. He couldn't do both. This place is a lot more than what your grandfather or Gerry had in mind. It's great."

"I think you're reading too much into this."

"No, I'm telling you the truth. You're a good dad. A good friend. Diane says you're a catch," he continues. "I wouldn't know, but I believe the wife. She's the smart one."

He touches the calendar on the wall. "We're always busy because every woman in Kentbury and the neighboring towns brings their cars here—just to see you. They'd kill to be Miss Lee. She's the one who's got your attention."

"She's just a friend." I stick to my standard line. In this town, any piece of information spreads like wildfire. He'll tell Diane who will call Mrs. Bowman and once she learns something, the entire town knows everything—with a spin, of course.

"I don't want to fuck-up our relationship."

"You're already screwing things up, boy. She's going to get tired of waiting. Pretty soon she'll leave your ass behind. How are you going to feel when you see her with another man?"

My heart begins to pound fast when he says the words out loud.

When Lee listed what she's missing and what she's looking for, I just stopped trying to persuade her on staying. I don't feel like I can compete with the man she deserves. When I hear Carson telling me about this other fictional man being by her side, it feels like a stab in the chest.

Losing her is inevitable unless I do something drastic.

But could she ever see me as something else?

Something more?

Would she care what I do?

I'm at a loss. Going to the library to get a book on how to run a business was easy. I bought *What To Expect During The First Two Years* when Cassie arrived at my doorstep. She's survived eight years and I don't suck at the parenting shit anymore.

Would there be something available that can tell me how to make this pain go away after a heartbreak?

Carson stares at me as if he's waiting for me to react.

I just say, "She's just a friend."

"You should watch Dr. Phil," he says. "My wife does religiously. He knows a lot about people and relationships."

"Carson, I don't need Dr. Phil."

"He'd say that you're in denial, my friend." He

ignores me. "You've been in love with that girl since she was Cassie's age. There's nothing you won't do for her. Do yourself a favor and get your head out of your ass before you lose her."

"I should fire you."

"My wife would still send me to work," he says without paying attention to my threat. "She thinks you're a good person who needs help running this place."

I check the clock and ask, "When are you leaving?"

"I'm staying until six in the morning. The cot in the office is ready, you should go to bed," he suggests. "Think about what you're doing. Gerry lost your mother because she wasn't a good fit for him. But Miss Lee is perfect for you, everyone in town knows it."

I rub the back of my neck and nod. "If you need me, call me. I'll be upstairs."

"You should be with Miss Lee," he calls out to me as I'm leaving.

Chapter Eight

Landon

I'VE SPENT many sleepless nights thinking of Lee.
Dreaming about her. Jerking off as I imagine her under
me, moaning as I thrust inside her sweet body. Nothing
calms the thirst. Tonight, it's worse. I'm restless as the
fear of losing her grips me by the throat.

Despite all my efforts, my heart has only belonged to
one person, Knightly Rose. Needless to say, I stay up all
night thinking about what Carson told me and how I'm
about to lose her.

The news that Mom dated my uncle blew my mind. I'm not surprised she left him because of who he was. My parents have always made sure that unless we follow their advice, everything we're doing isn't worthy of their approval.

Over and over we heard that my uncle was just a mechanic. A nobody who would never have what's needed to be happy. I guess subconsciously, I keep thinking the same about myself. If my parents can't see me as more than a dirty guy who makes a living by getting under hoods of cars, how would anyone else see me as more?

Lee's always believed in me. When she came to Boston for college, I had just lost my scholarship and she asked, "What are you going to do?"

"For now, I'm working at the garage down on Commonwealth Avenue, fixing cars and restoring motorcycles," I responded. "It's good money but not enough. Which is why I wait tables at O'Riley's Tavern."

"See, the world didn't end. MIT wasn't what you wanted, was it?"

I shook my head.

"You'll be fine, Miller. I have faith in you."

The only thing I lost when I had to leave MIT was my parents' respect. Which I only had for about a year or so anyway. Is it bad that I still smile when I remember those years partying? I enjoyed every moment. I was finally free from my parents and Kentbury. There was so much to do and experience that the classroom became secondary to me. I don't regret losing my scholarship, nor coming back to Kentbury and taking over the shop. I love what I do.

But that's not what defines me, who I am, or what I cherish the most in the world. Cassie and Lee are everything to me. Working hard not to ruin my friendship with Lee wasn't enough. She's leaving because I've been a coward and never gave her what's rightfully hers—my heart.

Around five in the morning, I go back to the garage to work on the Corvette and the cars I have to deliver this week. Once I'm done, I set a schedule for Carson. I email a list of the tasks I need everyone to do around the shop, in case I'm gone for the entire week. Lee's a simple and kind person. I'm sure that if we sit down and talk, we'll solve our relationship by the end of the day.

Once I'm done, I drive to Steve's with another change of clothes for Cassie. I'm hopeful that she'll agree to stay with him for another night. I need to have a long conversation with Lee, and I don't want anyone around while that's happening.

"Come on in before Bob escapes," he orders as he opens the door. "Lee took Cassie with her, along with a couple of liters of maple syrup."

I crack a smile. My kid got her wish, making candy this weekend. She always finds a way to persuade Lee.

Distracted by the news, I don't notice when Bob cannons toward me.

"Don't jump," I warn him, but it's too late, he springs on top of me. His paws settle on my chest.

"How are you boy?" I rub his ears gently.

He responds by licking my face. "Yes, it's good to see you too."

"I take it they left him since he can't be around while they make the candy?" I guess, pushing Bob away gently.

"Yep, Lee's kitchen must be a candy factory by now." He laughs. "You should go and catch up with them. Damian and Hops are there too."

Before I leave for Lee's house, I decide to check Carson's facts and ask, "Carson told me about Gerry and my mother. No one has ever said anything about it before."

I'm hoping he'll give me another version. Maybe there's no version at all.

"It's like everything in this town. Everyone talks about it as it happens," he says and shrugs. "The next thing you know, there's something new to keep the attention of the town and you forget all about it."

"So it's true?"

He nods and takes a seat in the living room. "Gerry always wanted to work in the shop. He didn't love your mom enough to quit and do something different. Just like she didn't love him enough to understand that cars were his passion. You're a lot like him. You have a gift with cars. Why would you waste your talent doing something else?"

"It's not a talent," I correct him. "It's just a trade."

"I've only met two people who can tell you what's wrong with an engine just by listening to it running. That's a gift," he insists. "Just like Lee. She knows how to make people feel at home. Each person has a talent, and they should embrace it."

"What do you think about her leaving for New York?"

He leans his head on the couch and takes a deep breath. "What's there to think? You're a father. You'll learn that as your children grow older, you can only be there to guide them, support them, and love them."

"I wish she'd stay," I breathe out the words. "I just don't know how to convince her that she can have everything she wants here. I'd work hard to give it to her."

"Finally. What took you so long?" His frustrated voice and his annoyed face remind me of Carson's attitude last night.

"Wouldn't you like someone better for her? I fix cars for a living, Steve. She deserves a lot more than me. Mom never gets tired of saying that I'm nothing as long as I work at the shop."

He shakes his head and tsks.

"Gerry was a remarkable man. One of my best friends. There's nothing he wouldn't do for his family, his friends, and his community. You're a lot like him," he continues. "He wasn't *just* a mechanic. I can see why you'd see yourself that way. His only flaw was loving your mother—and listening to her."

Steve straightens his back and clears his throat. "He could have moved on from your mother, but she made him feel undeserving. In my personal opinion, she can't see anyone happy—not even her children. My Rosie was the only person who put up with her. She used to say that everyone's special.

"You repair everything in this town, not only cars. Without you, the farm wouldn't run as smoothly as it does, nor the lodge, or the bed-and-breakfast. You created new jobs in our community when you took over the shop. The guys who come to you asking for a job don't know much, but you teach them everything you know. Whether they stay or not, you give them a future."

"I just do what Gerry used to do," I say, disregarding what he's saying.

Suddenly, it hits me. It's like I see everything in a different light. Steve is right, I always focus on what my mother says. I looked up to Gerry because I love him. Everyone respected him. I try to follow in his footsteps. That doesn't mean I should stay single because he wasn't good enough for the woman he loved—my mother.

Lee's nothing like her.

"Everyone is important in this world and certainly in this town. We're a part of the engine. If you're missing one piece, even if it's a small one, what would happen?"

"It'll work, but not properly," he answers me with a smile. "Earlier, I told Lee something similar. We can hire new people to take over her place, but she's the heart of our family. She matters in every way. Nothing will work as well, but we can function."

"Did you tell her to stay?" I ask hopefully.

"Did you ask her not to leave?" he retorts, giving me a challenging look.

"I wish I had done it before. It feels as if it's too late. I'm still not sure if I'm who she needs."

He sighs, exasperated. "We can spend an entire day talking in circles and never come to an understanding. Your parents aren't very supportive. It's hard to see things as they are when they keep making you feel like a failure. You're not. Everyone in this town looks up to you and cares for you. Lee deserves greatness. A man who supports her, protects her, and loves her. If you can't offer her that, then you're doing the right thing by letting her go. Don't try to hold on to her just because she's been kind to Cassie. Do it because she's who you want to spend the rest of your life with. Life is short," Steve says. "Too short, son."

He gets a faraway look about him. I don't know what to say. He sighs and continues.

"You never think the last time you kiss someone might be the last time," he says, his eyes dimming. He holds his head and shakes it. "One day I had everything and the next I got a call. Rosalinda died in a car accident. I was left with a baby girl and our two boys. I miss her every day, but we had a good life while we were together. Ten years of happiness.

"If you keep second-guessing yourself, you might be wasting precious time." He looks at me and says, "When you have the chance, you should never miss the opportunity to remind your loved ones how you feel about them. Don't miss the chance to kiss the love of your life. Always kiss deeper, harder, and fiercer than you think you can."

"Are you giving me your blessing?" I wonder.

"Well, no one is going to be good enough for her, but you're close enough." He smiles at me. "So, what are you going to do?"

Chapter Nine

Landon

CASSIE'S ALWAYS BEEN INDEPENDENT. Unless she's not feeling well, or she's sad. That's when she follows Lee or me around like a little duckling behind her parents. Today is definitely one of those days. She's clinging to Lee as if she were her lifeline. Of all the days that I need her to ignore us and beg to go outside.

"Sweetheart, why don't you go out and play?" I suggest.

She glares at me but doesn't say a word.

"There's plenty of snow to make snowmen," I try to persuade her.

"We already made a few at Grandpa's," Cassie answers, sternly.

"Should we go home?" I ask since the kitchen looks clean, and it doesn't seem like they're making any candy.

"No, I want to stay with Lee," she insists, wrapping her arms around Knightly's waist.

Kid, you're killing me. We don't have much time left before Lee leaves us. I have a non-established relationship to save. I stare at Damian and Bishop, who are here too.

"What are you doing here, Hops?" I ask exasperated.

It's like the entire universe decided to fuck with me this weekend.

"Chloe's packing her things. I don't want to be there," he explains.

Great, fucking great. "Shouldn't you be at your apartment, making sure that she's only leaving with her stuff?"

"Lee made sure to label everything earlier today," he explains. "The movers know not to take my things."

Will he ever grow a pair and stop depending on his baby sister? I glare at him.

"You seem edgy, do you want to hit the gym?" Damian proposes.

"Daddy, when can we go to the woods to choose the

Christmas trees?" Cassie looks at me. "Christmas is in two weeks."

I arch an eyebrow and exhale loudly, looking at Lee. "Probably next weekend. We'll have to coordinate with Grandpa and your uncles."

"Friday's good for me," Bishop says, checking his phone.

"We can discuss it later," Damian offers.

"Lee?" I bring her into the conversation because she hasn't said a word since I arrived.

She shrugs one shoulder and avoids my gaze. Fuck, if she was pissed yesterday, today she can't even stand me. I narrow my gaze when I notice her blotchy eyes. Has she been crying?

If Cassie weren't literally attached to her hip, I'd ask Bishop to take her for ice cream so I could be alone with his sister. I know my daughter, she's not going to leave Lee's side. If I try, I might make things worse. That's a risk I won't take today.

What happened to Cassie?

"Sunday," she mumbles. "I think Sunday might work."

"What's the plan for today?"

"I'm going to the gym," Damian says, standing up. "Do you want to come?"

"You should go with Uncle Damian," Cassie suggests. "Lee can take me home and put me to bed when it's time. She promised to read me a story."

"What have we told you, Cassie?" Lee presses her lips and gives her a chiding gaze.

My kid's so independent that sometimes she thinks she's old enough to make her own decisions. Lee and I keep reminding her that she's still a kid and has to follow the rules.

"Right, sorry," she apologizes and pouts. "Daddy, can I please stay with Lee, so we can make candy? If you want, she can take me home after dinner."

Lee kisses the top of her head. "Much better, sweetheart."

"If it's okay with you," Lee says, casually.

My two girls seem to be in a mood. Though I want to stay and make sure they're all right, I leave because it's clear that neither of them wants to do anything with me. Damian and I hit the resort's gym. We work out for about an hour. I take a shower, and then I go to his office to have dinner with him.

"Knightly mentioned that you're toying with the idea of buying the vineyard."

"It's a thought," he says with indifference, as if we're playing poker and he has an ace up his sleeve. "The McCalls want to move south. They brought it up to us, in case we want to make an offer."

"You don't have the cash flow," I remind him. "The resort is just starting to pay back what we invested."

"Do you want to back out from our agreement?" His nostrils flare.

"No, we have a deal. Actually, I want to stay in business together for longer than ten years—as per our current contract." I stop dancing around the subject. "We'll discuss it later though."

A couple of years ago, he came to me because the lodge was losing a lot of money. The rest of the family businesses were solid, but the hotel wasn't bringing in enough guests. If he renovated it and marketed it as a ski resort, he'd be able to turn it around. To do that, he needed my help. I had to convince Lee to sell the B&B and for her to focus on the other businesses.

I not only hated his plan, but I also wanted to break every bone in his body for even thinking about taking the Victorian house away from Lee. Instead, I lent him the money to renovate the lodge. I would be his silent partner for the next ten years. Once the contract expired, he'd pay me back—with interest.

Long term, it'd be more useful for my family if I keep that fifty percent ownership that'll pass directly to my kids. After all, we wouldn't break tradition, it would all stay within the family.

"What happened to, 'I'll be a silent investor'?" He glares at me.

"I'm keeping your secret, aren't I?"

"You're still butting into my business, and now you want to take the vineyard."

"Holden's retiring from the Airforce, he might want

to invest in that—and I'd help him. You're not financially stable enough to make that kind of move."

He swallows and stares at me for a couple of seconds. "I see. The hero comes back home, and you would have a cozy place for your big brother."

I nod and stare at him. What's his problem?

"If I acquire the vineyard, it'd be part of the family business," he explains as if trying to persuade me not to do it.

"Bishop and Lee would be part of it. Hops seems to like the idea since it'd be a perfect complement to the cider business," he says carefully. "We'd have to apply for a loan. Harris Estate is in good standing. We have assets."

"You can't put the resort up as collateral, nor the B&B," I remind him.

"It'll boost our business. We can sell cider to the liquor stores that buy the wine," he explains, agitated. "That's another push to help not only the Harris name but the town. What do you want from me, Miller?"

"To even consider including you in the vineyard transaction," I say, grinning, "you'd have to change some things. I'd no longer be a silent partner. You'll have to come clean to your siblings about my role in the resort. Last but not least, if, and only if, Holden is okay with that, we'll make you a partner in the vineyard."

"Since when did you become an asshole?"

I stand up, getting ready to leave. "The day you tried

to fuck with Lee. They're your family, not pawns to move around."

"You're supporting the wrong Harris. She's leaving." He grins with satisfaction.

I narrow my gaze, my mouth tasting like bile.

"Are you the one who pushed her to leave?" I fire the question, holding myself because I want to punch the grin off of his fucking face. "Did you do it so you can have her share of the estate?"

"No, but her leaving helps us," he responds with a victorious smile. "I can make a few changes to the house. You can only fit so many guests as it is now."

The fucker's going to add rooms and take away the historical element to the place.

"While she's in New York, she'll learn how to run a big hotel. I want her to run the resort."

Oh, fuck. Why didn't I see this yesterday? Whatever he used to play with her mind and get her out of here must be eating her up inside. Damian isn't a bad person, he's just too focused on his goals to pay attention to others.

I chuckle, rolling my eyes. "Enjoy your little victory dance while it lasts."

"What do you mean?"

"Lee's right, you can be so obtuse."

Chapter Ten

Landon

ON MY WAY to Lee's house, I stop by Carson's to give him instructions for the next week. There's no way I can convince Lee to stay today. First, I have to figure out what happened on Saturday. Then, I have to convince her to stay with me. Third, I need to do all this away from the family.

When I arrive home, Bishop and Lee are in the living room.

"Sorry for getting back so late," I apologize, shedding off my coat.

It's cold outside. The national weather service reported a freeze warning. Sometimes they're wrong, but if the humidity lingering in the cold air is any indication, we're going to have a bigger storm than they're predicting.

That translates into revenue for everyone in town. The reservations at the ski resort are going to triple by Wednesday. The same will happen with the Bed & Breakfast. My biggest worry is Lee, since she wants to drive to Manhattan tomorrow morning.

"It took you a long time." Bishop gives me a disapproving look. "Were you two fooling around with the guests?"

I sigh, seriously does he have to bring that up in front of his sister?

"Of course not, I was caught up in a meeting."

Lee frowns and stares at me for a long time. It's on the tip of her tongue to ask what kind of meeting, but she just says, "It's okay, Cassie's already in bed."

"Thank you, what was going on with her earlier today?"

Lee shrugs.

She doesn't respond and turns her attention to Bishop. "Are you ready to go?"

Hops nods, glaring at me.

What the fuck did I do to him?

"What time do you plan to leave tomorrow, Lee?" I ask as she puts on her snow boots.

"Around five in the morning," she answers, looking around for her hat. "If Cassie needs anything, call Dad or my brothers."

I nod and go to my room for the hat she forgot last week.

"Here." I put it on her and caress her delicate cheek with the back of my hand. "I'm sure the other hat will turn up later this week."

"Cassie might not have school tomorrow," Lee continues, stepping away from me. "Check with Dad or Hops if you need help."

"Please, don't worry about it. I have it covered. Thank you for today."

"Any time."

"Drive her carefully, Bishop," I request as they climb in his truck.

I go to Cassie's room to check on her. She's not in bed, but inside her tent with a book and her flashlight.

"Shouldn't you be in bed, young lady?" I try to feign anger, but I love when she hides in her secret place to read.

"Why is Lee leaving town?" She glares at me.

"Where did you hear that?" I sigh.

I'm not ready for this conversation.

"Grandpa Harry and Uncle Hops were talking about it," she explains. "I don't want her to go."

"It's just an interview," I say, trying to keep things real but not giving her any hopes, yet.

"I know, with the baby hospital," she says in a grown-up tone.

I blink twice and stare at Cassie. "What do you mean?"

"Uncle Hops said that she was going to buy guy's junk and have a baby in New York," she explains and lifts her hands while shrugging. "What's guy's junk?"

Fucking Bishop, how many times do we need to tell him to be careful of what he says around Cassie?

"I'm sure he didn't mean that," I mutter, astonished by the news.

My mind works hard trying to catch up with everything that's been happening this weekend. And suddenly, it freezes, and I just can't think anymore. Lee mentioned a family. A guy, kids, and a home.

Why would she just plan on getting pregnant?

"Then what did they mean?" Cassie stares at me with a challenging look.

Her hearing is perfect as well as her comprehension. She listens to every conversation and learns too fast. I don't want her to learn yet what "guy's junk" is. Certainly, when she learns, I want her to know the right words. Not Bishop's version.

"Why don't we ask Lee the next time you see her," I offer.

"That won't be until next Saturday. She's going to be leaving for a week." Her lower lip quivers when she says, "Dad, can we convince her to stay?"

"I can try." I play it down. "You have to go to bed."

"Grandpa Harry said that there's not going to be any school tomorrow," she protests. "He knows a lot about the weather."

Steve shouldn't have mentioned the weather to Cassie. He'll have to deal with the sleepy, grumpy kid tomorrow.

"We're not sure, sweetie, you have to go to bed." I don't budge.

She rolls her eyes and finally walks out of the tent and climbs onto her bed.

"Maybe we can buy a big house," she suggests. "Lee can live with us."

Just great, she's already planning our future, and I can't even think of how I'm going to convince Lee to let me take her on a date.

Cassie presses her lips together and moves her mouth from one side to the other. "Bob can sleep with me every night."

There's that little bonus to her plan, she's getting a pet too.

"I heard Uncle Hops say that she wants a home and a family," she continues.

At least now I understand why Cassie has been upset all day. She overheard that Knightly might leave Kentbury and wants me to fix it.

"Lee is our family, isn't she, Dad?" she asks with hopeful eyes. "You always say that. We can all live together." Then, she gives me a mischievous smile. "You two can have a baby. Remember what you told me?"

I hold my breath because I just can't with this kid and her ideas.

"When a mom and a dad love each other, they make babies. You love Lee, don't you? She's our Lee," she continues.

This kid is on a roll.

"And if she's a mom..." She pauses, looking at me seriously. "Well, she can be my mom too."

She gives me a sharp nod and smiles widely. It's like she solved the crisis. She stopped the end of the world.

"That's what I'm going to ask Santa for. To keep Lee with us and make her my mom."

I grab one of the frames that she has on her nightstand. It's a picture of Lee holding Cassie when she was only a month old. She stands right next to the Christmas tree at her father's house. The day my daughter came into our lives, Lee didn't just welcome her, she loved her from the first moment she held her.

"Let me worry about that, okay?" I kiss her forehead. "Your job this week is to be on your best behavior. Promise?"

She pushes herself up and jumps into my arms, hugging my neck. "I promise, but please, don't let her go. Santa doesn't always bring me what I want, I trust you more."

Chapter Eleven

Knightly

BISHOP AND DAMIAN have a list of instructions on what to do while I'm gone. It's just a week, but that's all the time they need to fuck up my guests, my gift shop, and their lives. Not that I should care.

When did I become the oldest of the three?

I swear, I was the baby. Now, they need me to hold their hands every single day. From this point forward, I'm just going to focus on me—well at least until next

Saturday. I'm sure while I'm in Kentbury, they won't leave me alone.

If everything goes as planned, I'll arrive in New York around ten or eleven. That should give me plenty of time to find a salon to fix my messy hair and maybe get my nails done. At three o'clock I have my appointment at the fertility clinic. It's just a consultation where the doctor will explain the process and the cost of going through artificial insemination.

On Tuesday, I have an all-day interview. If that goes well, on Wednesday, I'll have another round of interviews.

Damian doesn't like the idea of having a child without a father, but I want to know my options. Ideally, I would love to meet a guy and fall in love. But if that doesn't work, I can adopt or just have a baby.

"You got this, Lee, who needs fucking Landon Miller?" I say, dragging my bags toward the living room.

"I hope you do," he answers.

The man himself stands by the door, wearing his winter gear.

I need to start locking my door.

Where is he going?

"Why are you here?"

"There's a big storm coming. It's snowing already. But if we leave now, we might reach Manhattan before they close the roads."

"We?" I cross my arms, looking at him defiantly. "You're not coming with me."

"Lee, you drive like a pro. However, a blizzard is about to hit us. The roads are going to be bad, and neither your father nor I would be able to breathe knowing that you're out there alone."

He uses a dirty trick. My father and the snowstorm. Mom died in these same conditions. I was just three months old. I could fight him, but this isn't about him or me. It's about Dad.

"Okay," I yield.

He nods and walks toward me, taking my bags. "I'll load them in my truck. Let's go."

But as I'm about to step out of the house, I suddenly remember his kid. "Wait, what about Cassie?"

"Your Dad's already at my place. He's taking her for the week," he says reassuringly. "Everything is under control. We'll be away, enjoying New York for a week, and Kentbury will remain in one piece."

"This isn't a vacation, Miller," I warn him.

He gives me a smug smile and tilts his head. "We'll see."

I groan, he's so fucking infuriating.

THE ROADS ARE snow-packed by the time we cross the state line between Vermont and Massachusetts. Most of the cars are slowing down. Not us. Landon Miller doesn't believe in slowing down during a storm. We shouldn't linger around drivers who doubt themselves, those are the ones who cause accidents.

For me, it's unnerving to sit next to him while he's driving because I have to be quiet. The silence is slowly killing me. He has one rule. We don't talk when he's driving during a storm. It distracts him. Seeing that we have another three or four hours to go, I close my eyes, hoping to sleep for the rest of the trip. It's almost impossible. When we arrive in Hartford, Landon wakes me up, yelling, "Fucking asshole, get out of the road."

"Lovely," I grunt. "Good morning to you too."

"Sorry, I've been trying to control myself, but these fuckers are just getting on my nerves."

Needless to say, the next hundred miles are stop and go. We crawl along with the traffic. The no talking rule switches to swear words all the way to Manhattan. It's twenty minutes after one when we finally arrive at The Ambassador Hotel. It's new, it's trendy, and I'm not sure how I feel about it all, but I'm still excited to be here. I have less than two hours to eat lunch and find a Blow Dry Bar for my hair.

If I'm lucky, I can squeeze the visit to the nail salon after my appointment with the fertility clinic. If not … I look at my chipped, uneven nails. My nails will have to do with a nice clipping and a coat of the clear nail polish I have in my bag.

"Where are you staying?" I ask Landon.

"Hopefully, they have a room next to yours," he says, handing the bags to the bellboy. "I requested that when I made my reservations."

"You planned this?"

"I'd call it improvising," he corrects me and takes the ticket from the valet attendant. "Careful now, I know every inch of my truck, Frey."

The kid's eyes widen when Landon says his name. It's funny to see the reaction of people when he talks to them as if they're old friends. Most people forget they're wearing a name tag.

"Make sure it doesn't have a scratch, and I'll tip you well by the end of the week," he warns him in the friendliest tone he can use.

Landon is very particular about his cars. God forbid someone sees his Porsche Carrera. That thing is as old as my father, but according to Landon, it's a treasure.

I look at the kid who gives Landon a dismissive gaze.

"Seriously, don't scratch my car?"

Landon shrugs. "They need to learn to be careful with other people's stuff. Plus, maybe I can hire him to work at Jared's."

I give him an infuriating side gLandon and continue walking toward the entrance. He follows right beside me.

"Thank you for driving me even though it wasn't necessary. I'm sure Dad appreciates the gesture." I dismiss him as we enter the luxurious hotel.

There's a big Christmas tree right beside us, which reminds me that next weekend we're putting up the trees. It's going to be the last time I spend it with the Millers. Dad will have to drive from Vermont to spend the holidays with me. I'm not sure if Bishop would follow. Damian won't entertain the idea.

It's the high season, why would he waste his time celebrating something that's based on commercialized merchandise? We're lucky that he lives close by and takes a few hours to be with us. He's a combination between Mr. Scrooge and the Grinch. Sometimes he can be so fucking obtuse, cold, and heartless.

"Are you going to tell me why I've been on your shit list since Saturday?"

"There's no such list, and if I had one, you'd know why you're on it," I say, and then warn him, "I hope you have plans for the week. I'm going to be too busy to spend time with you."

Seriously, how can I find dates if I have this guy following me around? I double check my phone to verify that my profile is visible on Tinder. Bishop helped me open an account last night.

When I check in, the clerk asks me for my credit card. Only two out of the five nights I'm staying are paid by the hotel I'm interviewing with. Landon hands over his.

"Just put everything on my card."

I'm thankful that this isn't Kentbury or everyone in

town would know that Landon Miller's paying for my room. I groan. They already know that Landon and I are in New York, don't they?

"What's wrong?" Landon asks as we walk toward the elevator bank.

"Everyone in Kentbury knows we're in New York," I mumble. "I can just hear Mrs. Bowman, 'Cassie is lovely, but I'm glad you two had some alone time, dear.'"

I slap my palm on my forehead. This can't be happening.

"Let them talk, why would you care?"

I stab the number twenty several times until the doors close while glaring at him.

"You're hungry. Why don't we change clothes and have some lunch? I want us to talk," he suggests.

Food, yes, food sounds just about right.

I check the time on my phone. It's almost two. I barely have time to change and leave for my appointment.

"As I said, I have plans. My appointment is at three." I google restaurants near me.

Everything that pops up sounds fancy. I just want a slice of pizza. When the elevator doors open, he walks me to my room where the bellboy is already setting our bags.

"I'll be ready in five minutes," he says, tipping the guy that helped with our luggage. "We can find a place to grab a quick bite, and I'll get you to your appointment on time."

"You're not coming with me," I say but it's too late, he's already gone.

Chapter Twelve

Knightly

WHEN I REACH THE LOBBY, Landon's already waiting for me, holding a plastic bag.

"Here, I didn't find much, but this should do," he says, handing it to me.

"What is it?"

"Ham sandwich with extra mayo and provolone cheese," he announces.

When I open the bag, there's just one sandwich and a box of apple juice.

"What about you?"

"I ate mine while I was walking back to the hotel," he says casually before he asks the bellboy to get us a cab. "We can get something heartier after your appointment."

"Where are you going?" I glare at him as I slide into the cab and he does the same.

"I'm going with you, of course," he explains. "We need to talk."

"About what?" I huff and give the cab driver the address of the fertility clinic.

"You can't just walk away from your life to search for something you already have in Kentbury."

"Do we have to rehash Saturday's conversation, Miller?"

"Look, Cassie's devastated."

I knew it. Cassie wasn't going to let it go. She said last night that she understood. Instead of allowing me to talk things through with her, she decided to ask her dad to stop me. I love that kid, but seriously? As sweet as it is to know that this man would do anything for his daughter, I'm fuming. He just can't let things be, can't he?

"Fuck," he curses under his breath. "I upset you more, didn't I?"

"Landon, I'm sure your intentions are noble, but I'd appreciate it if you stop right now." I check the time. "This week is crucial to me. Thank you for driving me, I know that without you I might not have made it, but honestly, I'm not in the mood for another intervention."

He nods and stays quiet during the drive. Once we arrive, he pays the cab and helps me out of the car. The man keeps following me, even when I'm glaring at him.

"You can't go in with me."

"Why not?"

"This is a private consultation," I explain.

"What is it about?"

I ignore him and step out of the elevator. The reception area is right across from us.

"Knightly Harris," I announce to the receptionist. "I have a three o'clock appointment with Dr. Gonzalez."

She hands me a clipboard. "If you don't mind filling out that information. Most insurances don't cover the procedures, but we'll be happy to submit a claim on your behalf. Can I have your insurance card and driver's license?"

I give her what she asks for and take a seat to fill out my medical history. Of course, Landon just can't let things be.

"How do you know you have fertility issues?" He dares to ask.

"I'm not having this conversation with you, Miller," I say with a warning voice.

The steel door next to the reception opens, and a nurse calls out my name, "Knightly Harris."

I stand up and follow her. The infuriating man who

has decided to make my life miserable walks right behind me.

"After you finish filling out your information, give the clipboard to the receptionist," the nurse says, stopping right in front of an office.

"Please, take a seat. Dr. Gonzalez will be with you shortly."

She pulls a plastic cup out of her pocket and hands it to Landon. "If you decide to leave a sample on your way out, there's a room next to the reception. We have magazines and movies if you need them."

Landon moves the cup around, staring at it as if it's a strange, alien object.

"Write your name, her last name and your date of birth *before* using it," she emphasizes. "Once you're done, make sure to close it tightly."

His mouth agape and widened eyes break me out of my bad mood. I never thought I'd see Landon speechless.

"You can always get paid if you decide to make a donation," I say grinning.

"Are you having fun at my expense, Harris?"

"I could," I say, taking a seat. "It's not too late for you to leave. Things might get more interesting."

The doctor enters wearing blue scrubs, her brunette hair tied low in a ponytail, and her surgical mask hanging from her neck.

"Mrs. Harris, it's very nice to meet you. I apologize

for my attire, but one of my patients just went into labor, and I didn't have time to change," she says, shaking my hand and then offering it to Landon. "You must be Mr. Harris. It's a pleasure to meet you."

"Don't worry, thank you for seeing me on such short notice," I say.

"As my nurse must've explained to you, consultations are just casual chats. Though we'd love to help you achieve your dreams, sometimes we're not the right fit," she explains and fidgets with her mouse, then looks at us.

She takes her time studying us and asks, "How long have you been trying to conceive?"

"Conceive?" I frown.

"Getting pregnant is different for everyone. For some couples, it can take only a few tries while for others, they have to follow some steps. What kind of birth control have you taken in the past?"

I squint and stop answering the questionnaire they gave me at the entrance. "I haven't taken anything for the past five years."

She nods. "And you've been trying to get pregnant for the past five years?"

"No, this is new."

She beams. "I see. Mr. Harris, how old are you and have they checked your sperm count already?"

"I'm not—"

"He's thirty-four," I interrupt, taking advantage of this little interrogation to make him squirm or leave.

"But... things don't work well with him, if you know what I mean," I mumble.

Oh, he's going to pay.

"What are your symptoms?" She's super professional about this. Damn, I have to make it more uncomfortable for him.

"Are you having trouble getting an erection, or is it keeping it?" she asks, taking out a notebook and grabbing a pen. "How is your sexual desire?"

"I don't have any. This isn't—"

"Well, he doesn't like to talk about his... problem," I continue.

"I can assure you, we've heard everything." She beams with pride. "We can find the issue and work to fix it."

"Dr. Gonzalez, no offense but I bet you haven't encountered a problem like ours," he states and gives me a gentle squeeze.

"It's okay to be shy about your sex life. Infertility happens to everyone. But in this clinic, we have a solution for it," she continues. Nothing Landon tells her is going to stop her goal—getting us a baby. "Once we find the root of your problem, we'll establish a routine. Maybe you guys are too stressed out about having this baby. It happens. Whatever your problem is, we can solve it."

"Maybe you're right," he says, tossing his mischievous smirk at me. "What kind of routine do you recommend? Sex therapy?"

What is he trying to do?

He sets the cup on the desk. "I know I'm not the problem. I have a daughter, maybe we haven't tried hard enough."

She takes my hand and gently says, "Have you tried to relax, dear? I think you two need to talk about this and agree on how you're going to proceed."

Dr. Gonzalez stands up and goes to her cabinet.

"There's a lot of myths out there, for example, Mr. Harris do you masturbate?"

"Do you, Landon?" I look at him with interest. "Because you might run out of sperm before I can use it."

She chuckles. "Don't be silly. Actually, if you don't do it, start doing it often. The way your body produces the sperm is based on demand."

"You can help him," she says. And I swear I can't understand how she can keep a straight face when she says, "Masturbation is a healthy activity, and when done with a partner, it helps you grow as a couple."

"Shouldn't you be taking notes, Lee?" Landon winks at me. "The sooner we start, the faster we can come to a happy ending."

"How are your drinking habits?" she continues ignoring my annoying friend. "I recommend that you limit your intake to no more than two servings a day."

"I need you to stop smoking, using steroids, get tested

for STDs, and don't wear skinny jeans." She hands him a couple of booklets.

"Here's the complete list of recommendations for the two of you. You should see a marriage counselor too. Therapy works wonders when you're too stressed out about having a kid." Dr. Gonzalez looks at me with a straight face and says, "Sex therapy is a great idea."

"Look at this, honey." He shows me the illustration of a couple having intercourse. "The Kamasutra, fifteen positions to get pregnant. Hmm. I never thought about this, doggy style. We could do it in the kitchen."

My cheeks heat up when I think about us having sex in my kitchen. But I stop because he's just taunting me.

"Landon," I warn him.

"The Anvil position," he continues. "I'm glad you do yoga. With your elasticity, we can get very creative."

"It seems like there are things you two haven't tried yet," Dr. Gonzalez continues. "Sex can be fun. It's not just about having a set schedule."

"Darling, we'll make it fun," Landon promises, taking my hand and kissing my palm. "We don't need doctors or test tubes to make a baby. Just two willing parties."

He winks. "I'm willing."

I'm not sure if he's making fun of me, but I'm tempted to ask him to do it in the cup so I can have a baby. It'd save me twenty thousand dollars, and I'd know where the kid has come from.

"I'm here to help with whatever you need, but I think it's important for you two to relax. Remember the love that you have for each other. It's not just about conceiving but loving each other."

"We'll try your techniques," Landon says as he continues to look at the booklet that she gave us. "Maybe we'll send you a Christmas card with the picture of Junior and Cassie."

"That would be lovely," she says satisfied, thinking that she just solved our problems.

Lady, you can't even see the tip of the iceberg.

"Give yourself the next four cycles, if you haven't conceived by then, I recommend you start by visiting your obstetrician—we're your last resource."

Landon sighs and fans the booklets that she gave him. "My boys will know how to get the job done, Doctor, but thank you for the information. We can start practicing now."

"Thank you, Doctor," I say, lost in thought, wondering how exactly I'm going to ask him to do it in a cup so I can knock myself up.

Chapter Thirteen

Landon

WE LEAVE the doctor's office in silence. I hope I didn't piss her off more than she already was.

"Here are my forms," Lee mumbles at the receptionist.

"How much do we owe you?" I ask, pulling out my wallet.

"The first consultation is free," the receptionist explains. "Would you like to schedule another appointment?"

"Not at the moment," Lee says, lost in thought.

She's either upset because her little game of "let's make Landon squirm in his seat" didn't work, or she didn't like that the doctor didn't give her the information that she wanted.

We step into the elevator, and as the doors close, I say, "Go out on a date with me."

While she simultaneously asks, "Would you mind being my sperm donor?"

"I'd do anything for you, Lee. Giving you a baby would be an honor, but why don't we start with a date?"

"Why would you want to go out on a date with me?" She gives me a defiant glare.

"Because I find you attractive, I care about you, and I think we'd have a good time," I say, hoping that I'm saying the right words because one slip and I'll be out of her life.

She studies me, looking at me from top to bottom and says, "Why now?"

"What do you mean why now?" I stare at her in confusion.

"We've known each other for a long time," she explains. "Years. Why would you want to change the dynamic now?"

"Why not?"

"What's the goal?"

"I want to change our relationship," I confess.

"You're my best friend, but I don't want to be *just* your friend."

Lee shakes her head. "You want me to believe that you want more."

"No, it's not about believing, but just moving forward," I say with conviction.

"Why are you doing this?"

Asking her out isn't enough. I study her, trying to understand her guarded gaze.

"Because I want to go out with you," I explain, choosing the simple answer. "I want us to be a real couple who fight about the toothpaste, the toilet lid, and who's feeding the dog early in the morning."

"Just like that?" She glares at me. "You want us to be a couple? Does this have anything to do with Cassie not wanting me to leave Kentbury?"

"What do you mean?" I frown confused.

"She offered me your room if I wanted to move into a new place."

"Well, obviously we'll have to buy a house." I agree with Cassie's assessment. "Your dog takes over an entire room."

"So, let me get this straight. Cassie told you that I'm leaving. She doesn't like it and you're trying to fix it for her," she says, her hands on her hips and her chin tilted. "But I bet that's just the tip of the problem. You don't like the idea that the help is leaving. My father must've told you some sob story about my place in Kentbury and how you should stop it."

"You're wrong," I protest.

"So, Cassie didn't ask you to stop me from moving to New York?"

I swallow hard and stare at her. How do I explain to her that even though Cassie doesn't want Lee to leave, I'm here for myself?

"Did she or did she not?" She taps her shoe against the hardwood floor.

"That's not why I'm here."

She huffs. "You're one of the best dads in the world. It's cute to see you work with her in the garage, explaining to her how every wrench works. Let's not forget how heart-melting it is to watch you guys go on Daddy-and-me dates. There's nothing you wouldn't do for her, including trying to stop me from leaving."

"Can we forget about Cassie for one moment and talk about us?"

"Landon, I can't toy with the possibility of dating you. It'll never work. I'm just Lee, your friend."

She fixes her scarf and leaves the building. I follow right behind.

"Damn it, Lee. You're not only that. Can you listen to me, please?" I call a cab before she starts walking back to the hotel or leaves me behind.

During the drive, she remains silent. Once the driver stops, she flies out while I'm paying. I have to run to catch up with her. She's trying to lose me, but I won't let her. I have to plead my case and beg her for a chance.

"Can we please talk about our situation?" I insist.

"We don't have a situation, Landon," she clarifies.

"Because you're shutting down all the possibilities," I blame her.

"Are you going to tell me that you grew feelings for me overnight?" She rolls her eyes.

"Feelings don't grow overnight, but I can hide them for years," I tell her.

"Look, I've had my heart broken almost every day for the last eighteen years. First, it was Marcia Newton."

"What about Marcia Newton?"

"She was your first kiss, not me." Her low voice breaks.

"Then, it was the string of girls you dated while you were in high school," she continues, hunching over, almost choking a sob.

My heart slows down as I witness the pain I've put her through. If I had known I was hurting her, I swear to God I would have stopped.

"I moved to Boston and what did I find? A revolving door of nameless women. Just when I thought things might work out between us because we were both going to live in Kentbury, I discovered that you had a new hobby—the guests at the lodge. It was hopeless. I should've moved on, but eight years ago, you found me alone at the creamery. I was a little depressed. Mark was getting married."

"You said you didn't love him," I growl, and until now I've never let myself be fucking upset about that bastard.

"I didn't. I was sad because he proposed to me first. It stung that he moved on. It hurt that I couldn't love someone who would want a future with me, and I was pining for a guy who would never see me. That night, you said I deserved more than Mark. I was smart, beautiful, and I had a good heart."

She looks at her left hand and then at me. "For a moment, I thought you could finally see me. A couple of weeks later, Cassie arrived, and I kept being your buddy."

"Lee, I'm so fucking sorry," I apologize, but the words aren't enough.

"You're here because Cassie believes that you can fix everything. Dad thinks you can persuade me to go back if you say just the right words."

"They have nothing to do with me being here," I assure her.

"Bishop keeps telling me to confess my feelings so I can move on with my life," she continues. "Well, here they are, out in the clear."

She pulls back her shoulders and looks me in the eyes. "I've been in love with you since I was fourteen. I waited for you because I thought one day, you'd see me.

You'd notice me and you'd love me as much as I love you. But you don't have to worry about me. After almost eighteen years, I'm done with this unrequited love."

"Lee." I swallow hard as I realize how much pain I've inflicted on her, when all I've tried to do is protect her.

"It's okay, I'm a big girl," she says, dismissing me. "I made up my mind. If it's not this job, I'll find something else. I'm not going back. The only thing I need to have is a baby. Look at you, you've done well as a single dad."

Knightly's a patient woman. She's a saint when it comes to waiting for things to happen. But when she runs out of patience, she's done. Nothing and no one will change her mind. Thank you, fucking Damian. He pushed the right buttons to get her out of Kentbury. It's going to take a miracle to convince her that maybe she's been waiting since she was fourteen, but I've loved her for longer.

Sure, it seems like I'm a great dad. Everyone praises my skills, but none of them look closely enough to notice that my daughter's being raised by Lee too. She doesn't miss having a mom because she's had Knightly her entire life. We're a team. We've been a team since the first night Cassie came into our lives. And when we're at a loss, her family is there for us.

I've been so fucking scared to mess up what I have with Lee, that I didn't do the right thing from the beginning. Moving forward, I have to be clear about my feelings, which is so fucking hard. How do I do that?

I remember the first night with Cassie when I had no idea what to do with her. Lee said, *just love her. Just show her how much she means to you. As long as she feels loved, everything else is secondary.*

It's the same concept, right?

"I can see why you won't believe me." I weave my words wisely. "Anything I say might feel hollow. You'll think that Cassie, Steve, or your brothers pushed me to follow you and drag you back home."

"Didn't they?"

I can tell her Damian's plans, and she'll be on a plane to Kentbury to kick his ass. That won't solve our lives.

"I'm here for myself. Last Saturday night, I had a hard time breathing when you said you were leaving. It felt as if someone was ripping my heart out of my chest. I need you by my side to feel alive. My life revolves around you and Cassie. You two are my world. Give me a week to show you I can be the man you deserve."

"What does *the man you deserve* even mean?"

"You're Knightly Harris. One of the prettiest girls in Kentbury. You're smart, went to college, and you're the daughter of Rosalinda Kentbury—the last Kentbury. Simply put, you're unattainable."

Damian and Knightly have a few things in common.

Like the darkened eyes, the flaring nostrils and the twitching jaw when they get upset.

"I've worked overtime to hide any emotions that you provoke. Every day, I remind myself that you're my friend—my *best* friend. Overstepping would only put our relationship at risk. It's fucking hard, but I can't lose you. You're too important to me."

"I wish I could believe you," she says.

"One week," I plea. "Give me this week. If, by Friday night, I can't change your mind, I'll give up and give you what you want. A baby."

"You'll give me a baby and you'll walk away?" She squints and crosses her arms.

"Well, kind of," I say honestly. "I'd want to be a part of his life. I mean, fuck, Lee he'd be ours. I can't just walk away from him, and Cassie wants a brother." *And you as her mom.*

"I'd be living in New York."

"Your life is in Kentbury."

"It *was* there. If I'm going to unfall in love, I have to be away from you."

I finally breathe. The good news is that she's still in love with me. The bad news is that she's making up shit. What the fuck does unfall mean? That's not even a word.

"One week," I repeat, ignoring the ridiculous word she made up. "Just give me until Friday night, please. You take down those walls. We don't hide from each other."

"Aren't you afraid that afterward, things will be weird between us?"

"Weirder than these past three days? That's impossible," I state and take her hand. "You're determined to leave and move on, I have only one request. For the next week, let me show you what we can be."

I'm not sure if what I'm saying is romantic or even makes sense. She might be wanting to hear something more heart-stopping.

She looks at me, stunned. "Five days?"

I nod and wait. The silence stretches from seconds to maybe minutes.

The wait feels eternal.

Then, she tilts her head and narrows her gaze.

"If it doesn't work, you give me a baby?"

I fan the booklets they gave us at the clinic. "I would go through the entire Kamasutra for you. But I would like to explain that when you're ready, we won't need any fancy positions to get pregnant. I don't drink much. I'm clean, but if you want, I can get tested."

I caress her face, stepping closer to her. I bend down and kiss her cheek lightly. My gaze draws to her full, parted lips pulling me to her.

"Give me time to win your heart, Lee," I plead my case.

"Landon." My name sounds like a weak gasp as I caress my mouth with hers.

Our eyes lock, and our souls fuse.

"This is how we'll do it. I hand you my heart," I whisper. Our lips are so close, I can feel her tremble with longing. "I'll take care of the rest," I finish, tasting her lips as I cup the back of her neck.

She threads her hands through my hair.

I kiss her gently, deeply, possessively, with a fervent urge. My heart beats faster. I always knew that if I ever kissed her, it'd be like touching heaven. But the reality is beyond my wildest dreams. "Five days, please," I ask again, resting my forehead on top of hers and trying to recover my breath.

She doesn't respond but gives me a slight nod. I hate that she's not trusting me.

Chapter Fourteen

Knightly

HE KISSES me like I've never been kissed before. Like his entire life depends on just this one moment. I want him to stop because his taste is intoxicating. If this continues, I'll become addicted to it. One thing I've learned after all this time is that there's no worse feeling than not knowing if I should wait or forget him.

"Five days, please," he insists as his forehead rests on top of mine.

My chest is tight, and my throat feels like it's closing in.

It's just anxiety, Lee, breathe through it.

Ha!

As if it's so easy to breathe through a major life change when one doesn't even know what, precisely, is about to change. I'd like to reset the timer, go back to Friday or Saturday and reboot them. Start anew and ignore my brothers. No, I should go back in time thirty-five years and make sure that Damian and Bishop don't hit their heads so many times.

This is all their fault.

Wait, if I go back that far, I might be able to meet my mom. At the thought of my mother, I remember my sweet Cassie. How will she feel if I date her dad? If things don't work out, she's going to be crushed. If Landon gives me some of his boys and I have a baby… They can't live apart. She's already growing up without a mother.

"Lee, what's going on in that head of yours?"

"This won't work," I conclude. "Have you thought about Cassie?"

"For the next five days, it is just the two of us. We're not going to think about Cassie, your family, or the town," he says, grasping both my arms gently with his hands as his light blue eyes connect with mine. "You're afraid, I understand."

"Do you?" I challenge him. "Because I don't under-

stand myself anymore. And then there are the conse-
quences. It's easier if I just move away and find a new
life. What you're proposing changes the lives of a lot of
people."

"Moving here shifts the entire landscape of Kentbury. Your departure would alter my life, who I am, and
my future," he says in a desperate tone. "I'd be hollow
for the rest of my life."

"You'll be fine," I reassure him with the same words
I've been repeating inside my head since I decided to
come to New York.

"You know that I suck at relationships. You've seen
my role models. Both of them seem to be missing
emotions and a heart. I'm afraid to lose what we have,
which is why I never dared to think beyond our friendship," he explains in what seems a desperate attempt to
convince me that what he's done in the past is to save us.
"I can't afford to lose you."

"Why now?"

"I can't deal with the idea of not seeing you every
day, of not listening to your voice, or looking at your
beautiful face. You have this magical power to make
everyone feel special. When you're next to me, I feel
invincible."

"You can still lose me," I say, skeptical about the situation and his change of heart.

He nods. "At least a few years from now, when you
visit Kentbury with your new family, I'll be able to say I

gave it my best—and I'm happy because you're happy."

His words take my breath away. They're perfect. Each one filled with sadness and yet, a hint of hope.

"This week will be one of my most cherished memories," he concludes.

I fight the tears, but a few escape. He clears them with his thumb and asks, "What's the matter?"

"What you said reminds me of Dad. He loves Mom so much he's never moved on. When we ask him, he always says he has us. We're the best part of the two of them. He doesn't need more. One day, they'll find each other in heaven where they can be together again —forever."

I use the sleeves of my shirt to wipe my eyes. "That's the kind of love I want."

He takes me into his arms, rocking me from side to side. "Stay with me, Lee. Let us be whatever we're supposed to be. Don't fight us."

DATING LANDON SEEMS LIKE A DREAM. Dreams can come true, but what if I wake up in the middle of the perfect kiss and get hit by the rawness of reality? He's just a friend.

I want to believe in the magic of love, soul mates, and Landon Miller.

Maybe I should, but it's hard to believe after so many years. Landon has never let me down. I should trust him. He's never promised more than being there for me when I need him. And he's always there. Sun, rain, or in this case, snow.

Five days he asked for, and when I told him I had the interview tomorrow, he wasn't pleased. He felt like I was already giving up.

The job interview isn't about him. It's about me. I don't want to look back on my life in twenty years' time and wonder about the things I avoided or let go because I stopped putting myself first. Like getting this job at The Ambassador. I'm going to continue the process because I want options. Or at least, I'll show myself that I'm capable of doing more than running the B&B and the gift shop while making sure that my brothers don't ruin our legacy.

Landon isn't thrilled about my decision, but he understands and supports me. Tonight, we're going out on our first date—after I fix my hair and hopefully my nails. Once he leaves the room, I call the front desk to see if they have any appointments open at their spa and salon. While waiting for them to answer, I browse through their menu of services. I might ask for a lavender and cucumber wrap massage later this week. Thankfully, they can squeeze me in to do my hair, but not my nails.

While I'm on my way to my appointment, I text Damian.

Lee: We should add a spa in the resort and have Karla Olson run it.

He doesn't answer. I forget about him while I get pampered. We can talk about the family business next weekend. After a couple of hours, I feel like a model. It's been too long since the last time I got a haircut, let alone had my hair done by a professional. Karla, the town's stylist, only cuts it and sends me on my merry way. When I reach the elevator bank, my phone vibrates inside my purse.

Damian: She has her own salon, why would she want to do that?

Ugh, why can't he answer my texts when I send them.

Lee: We'd be offering services that she doesn't have in her salon, like massages, facials, wraps, and many more. We'll have the menu on our webpage. Pair them up with couples' weekends at the B&B.

Damian: I don't like the idea, not for the resort. We can reno-vate the B&B and add a wing with a couple of extra rooms.

Lee: We don't touch the Victorian house—it's a historical building.

I huff and push the elevator button. Then I text Landon.

Lee: I'm almost ready.

Landon: Take your time, text me when you want me to pick you up. Our reservation is at seven. Do you want to skate at Rockefeller Center tomorrow?

Lee: Maybe, can we decide that tomorrow?

Landon: They have a VIP service; we'd have to buy the tickets today.

Lee: Yes, I'd love to. Maybe next time we can bring Cassie with us.

Damian's text comes right after I send the one to Landon.

Damian: The spa won't bring any new customers.

Of course it will. Who wouldn't want to book a girls' weekend in Vermont and be pampered at our state-of-the-art spa?

Lee: We can discuss it when I'm back. It wouldn't happen overnight, but we should start planning.

Damian: You're leaving, remember?

Lee: Bishop, you can butt into the conversation whenever you want.

Damian: He's at Dad's, helping him with Cassie. Let things be.

Lee: You're not the only one who can decide what to do with the resort. We each own a fourth of it.

If I can convince Dad and Bishop, whatever Damian thinks is obsolete.

Damian: More like you and Dad own a fourth and the other fifty gets to decide what we do, but we can talk about that later. I'm on a conference call.

Wait, there's one fourth missing on that equation…

Lee: BISHOP did you sell your part of the resort to Damian?
I swear, I'm going to kill them.

Hops: I didn't sell it, I exchanged it for his part of the cider mill. It's just a ten-year deal so he could renovate it. We all win.

Lee: You're the only one who wins. No wonder he has no say around the orchard and the cider. What about the vineyard?

Hops: Are we buying it? It'd be perfect to market the cider.

Lee: We can have tours, wine tastings, and weddings. The spa would benefit from it. There's a perfect place where we can build the spa instead of adding it to the resort.

Damian: Stop, you two. We can't afford the vineyard.

Lee: It's a good move, there's so much we could do with it during the summer. You said it could happen.

Damian: We can't afford it at the moment, and I don't think we can get a loan. The Victorian house is under your name, and the resort can't be used as collateral.

Lee: So we can't add a spa, and the vineyard is a no go? I demand to see the books of the resort. I'm sure Dad would like that too.

Damian: I saved the place, you have no right to demand the books because you think we're in trouble.

Lee: When were we in trouble?

Damian: Lee, stop micromanaging. When you come back, we can sit down and discuss everything that I had to do to renovate the place. Maybe you'll agree to restore the B&B.

Lee: Over my dead body, Damian. That's a piece of history, leave it alone.

When I arrive at my floor, Landon's leaning against

the door of his room. My stomach becomes a big knot, and the frantic race of my heart barely allows me to hear when he asks, "Are you okay?"

The need for a kiss ceases as I wonder how he knows I'm not.

My phone vibrates again, and I decide to shove it back in my purse.

I sigh and shake my head. "As soon as I find out what Damian did with the resort, I'm going to kill him—and whoever helped him."

"You look beautiful," he says, cupping my face and kissing my lips. "Let's go for dinner before you start thinking about our funerals."

"Our?" I narrow my gaze. "Did you help him?"

"I like to think that I helped *you*, not just him. We can sit down and discuss it when we're back home. This week is all about pleasure, no business. Get ready." He kisses my nose and heads to his room.

Chapter Fifteen

Landon

WHEN LEE OPENS the door to her room every thought in my brain goes up in flames. Heat shoots through me. I'm gripped by raw lust. Lee's one of the most beautiful women I've ever seen. Tonight, she looks even more beautiful. She's wearing a little black dress snugged just perfect against her feminine curves. She wears a pair of four-inch heels accentuating her incredible, long, shapely legs.

Every coherent thought flies out of my brain.

Her hazelnut, silky hair flows over her shoulders. I want to reach out and slide my hands into it. Just once, I don't want to do the right thing when it comes to Lee. Instead of taking her on a date, I want to spend my time exploring her naked body. I can't stop myself, I snake an arm around her waist and press her against my body. I bend down and take her mouth.

"You look great," I say, gasping for air as I peel my lips away from hers. "Truthfully, more than great. Astonishing."

"You don't look so bad yourself, sir," she says play-fully. "You had those clothes hiding in your duffle bag?"

"I improvised," I explain. "The restaurant where I found the reservation has a jacket-required dress code." There are a few shops in the mezzanine of the hotel where I found a pair of slacks, a dress shirt, and a blazer.

"This is the second time in my life that I've seen you wearing something formal," she says, covering her mouth as she tries to stifle a chuckle. "The first time was at my graduation."

"Are you amused?"

"Just remembering that day. You looked dashing, except for your tennis shoes."

"Hey, I tried my best," I say looking down at my shoes.

At least I'm wearing a pair of boots today. They don't clash like the royal blue sneakers I wore that day.

"So where are we going?" she asks as we march toward the elevators.

"The Sky Riser," I inform her.

"The restaurant on top?" she asks with starry eyes.

Since it's snowing hard, I requested a table in one of the hotel's restaurants. The Sky Riser is the only one that had availability on such short notice. If given a choice though, I'd rather order room service, champagne, strawberries, and ice cream. I'd start the night by peeling off the little black dress she's wearing. I want to know what's under it. Some lace and silk, or just her silky skin?

Not today, Miller.

Lee's palpable excitement stops me from spoiling the perfect date.

"What are you thinking?" She looks at me suspiciously. "I'm pretty good at reading you, but I've never seen that face."

"You don't want to know," I say, pulling her into the car as the elevator's doors slide open.

I push her toward the metal wall, pressing my body against hers. "At least not yet."

I take her mouth and kiss her hard. Fuck, I'm never going to get enough of her. I'm lost in her, wishing to do more but I manage to stop. I have to set boundaries. Though, I don't know where I'm going to find the strength to withhold the urge to drag her to my room and make her mine.

"We have to stop." I groan, barely remembering my

own name and am surprised by the roughness of my own voice.

For a long moment, we look at each other. She's breathing as rapidly as I am. Her eyes are so dark I can't see her pupils.

"Somehow, I don't think you believe your own words, Mr. Miller." She gives me a cheeky smile.

I stroke her cheek with my thumb. "Have I told you you're beautiful?"

"No," she says, her face softening. "We can order room service," she proposes with a suggestive voice.

"Maybe on Wednesday. Today I'm taking you on a proper date," I say, fixing my jacket and my pants as the elevator reaches the top floor.

Chapter Sixteen

Knightly

Sparks fly all around us. It's like fireworks burst between us. The desire to have his hands all over me increases. Dinner be damned; take me to my room. The urge I feel draws me closer to him.

"Penny for your thoughts?" he asks.

Landon gLandons at me as we wait for the hostess to show us to our seats.

"Just a penny for all of them?" I say, still catching my

breath from our kiss. "There's a lot going on in my mind."

Especially how I can't seem to grasp this moment. My stomach is tied into a big knot and my heart races frantically. I'm on a date with Landon Miller, and instead of having something smart to say, I'm just focusing on his strong hands and his muscular arms. I stare at his broad, powerful shoulders encased by a formal jacket. He's always attractive but now, looking at him dressed formally is unsettling.

"That's a lot of energy wasted," he says with a low, dark velvety voice that slides down from my ears and hits right between my legs.

And he has to throw me that sexy, stupid smirk that makes my insides curl and my ovaries explode. It's the sensual curve of his mouth and the things I bet he can do with those lips.

"What can I do to make you forget home?" He interrupts my daydreaming with his rough voice. "If you want to talk about what's going on with the resort, I can tell you what I know. As long as you promise to put it on the back burner for the rest of the trip."

I sober up at the mention of the resort. Why in the world would my brother want me far away when he's in trouble?

"Why did he go to you?" I start with the basic question. "Don't get me wrong, I get it. You're his best friend.

Like Hops and I, we'd rather call you first than call our siblings."

He takes my hand, his calloused fingers caressing the inside of my wrist, making me shiver.

"Between the state-of-the-art resort they opened in Stowe and Airbnb, the bookings dropped dramatically," he explains.

"Why didn't he tell us?"

"You'll have to take that one up with him," he says, but I'm positive he knows the answer to it.

"Like he'll answer. He thinks he knows everything. Every time I make a suggestion, he shoots it down, like the spa," I protest. "And now he owns fifty percent of the place, which means he's going to ignore any ideas that I bring to the table."

He shakes his head. "I own fifty percent of the resort."

My eyes widen, and I forget how to breathe. Damian didn't dare sell the resort. We have rules, a tradition to follow.

"How?" I ask angrily. "He sold it to you?"

"Yes, but in ten years he can buy me out by paying off the loan with interest," he explains.

I straighten my back, set my hands on the table, and speak with my best business voice. "The changes we've done so far are working. If we add the spa, it'll bring guests all year round. We can sell it as a couple's weekend, a girls' weekend, you name it. And the vineyard next door is the cherry on top."

"You're adorable," he says, both dark brows furrowed right in the middle. "We're not talking business, Knightly Rose."

"Harsh, full name throwing doesn't look good on you, handsome." I try to smooth things over. "Think of this as an investment. I'm sure you're getting some kind of revenue while you own the place."

"Tomorrow I have a conference call with Holden about the vineyard. I'm going to see my financial advisor and my lawyer too," he continues. "I'm not saying yes to anything, but know that you'll be at the table when we start making decisions about the future of the vineyard, and everything will be taken into account."

"I don't understand why Damian would do that, sell part of our heritage." I try not to sound annoyed or resentful. It's impossible.

"It was in serious trouble." He sounds hurt. "He was at the point where if he didn't do something drastic, he would lose the lodge. In the larger scheme of things, that's the part of the Harris Estate that used to bring the most revenue. You lose it, and the other two aren't that far behind."

"Damian was looking at the big picture," he says. "If something has to go, it'd be the B&B."

My blood freezes when he tells me that Damian

wanted to sell it, but a rush of relief and comfort warm me up as I realize what Landon did.

"You saved my B&B," I state, staring into his blue eyes. "Is that why the deed is now under my name?"

He nods. "No one can touch it. It's your life."

Ever since Cassie came into his life, he's been working hard and finding ways to make a living for both of them while growing the business. He has a financial planner—one of his customers who lives in New York—who has helped him diversify his portfolio and make sure that Cassie has a comfortable future.

"I'm touched, but you have to think about Cassie and your future. Why would you risk your money on a place that might go under?"

"Because the B&B is yours. That's been your dream since you were little. There's no way I'd let anything happen to it. I always take care of my girls."

Landon's actions, words, and gestures are melting my heart. It's true, he's always taken care of his girls. That's what he calls Cassie and me.

"Please tell me this didn't tamper with our relationship," he says with an urgent and desperate tone.

Landon's a confident man. The few times he lets his vulnerability show is around me, and it's usually about Cassie.

"I swear I did it because—"

"You don't like when he tries to take advantage of me," I interrupt him.

It's just like the time when I was ten and I came back from trick-or-treating with my friends, and Damian confiscated my candy. Later that night, Landon brought back not only most of the loot Damian had taken away from me, but he went with Holden from door to door to get me more.

And if possible, I fall in love even more.

"Are our five days still on?" he asks hesitantly.

"Swoon me away, noble sir."

Chapter Seventeen

Knightly

IT's so easy to lose track of what we have when it's right in the palm of our hand. In just a few days, I've come to remember that I live in paradise. It's colder in Vermont than it is in Manhattan. That's one point to NYC. But nothing compares to the snowy mountains, blue skies, and the picturesque views of the town nestled between a curtain of firs.

The buildings towering around us aren't as appealing. I accept that I'm taken by the bright lights adorning the streets. There's a holiday feel, but it's not as intense or as inviting as the one we have in Kentbury.

The ice rink at Rockefeller center is okay, maybe even cute. It's nothing like the beauty of our big lake in Kentbury, skirted by the vineyard and a few cabins, and filled with a peaceful silence. We don't have big lines of people waiting for their turn to skate for just an hour on the lake.

"Are you sure you're going to be okay?" Landon asks as I shiver.

Cold oozes through the soft cashmere sweater I wear.

A couple of layers should be enough, I said as I got dressed.

This is nothing compared to Vermont's winter, I assured myself as I left the hotel room.

Don't be a wimp, Lee, I chide myself as a sting of cold air hits my face.

"Do you need my jacket?" Landon offers, his eyes creased at the corners.

"Nah, as soon as we're skating, I'll warm up," I insist as we enter the VIP area. "So why exactly did we pay more than a hundred dollars?"

"Well, you won't be freezing outside while you wait for your turn," he explains, taking me into his powerful embrace and rubbing his hands on my back to warm me up.

I look up at him. His heavy-lidded gaze assesses me. "You're beautiful," he whispers.

Landon cups my face with one hand and lowers his

head. I slide my arms around his neck and raise myself to meet him. My eyes drift shut when his mouth captures mine, his tongue flicks inside. My knees weaken. My heart gallops in my chest. The touch sends shivers of desire through my body, replacing the cold with a wildfire that warms every cell of my body and threatens to melt the entire city.

He kisses me gently. Slowly. Deeply.

I don't think I'll ever get tired of this. If anything, I would give everything to be kissed by Landon Miller for the rest of my life.

"Next," someone yells, breaking the spell.

Landon tears his mouth free, groaning in protest. His breathing is heavy, just like his gaze.

"I want to go back to the hotel," I request.

"What?" he asks in a gravelly voice.

"Sir, you're next," someone keeps calling us but at the moment, nothing matters.

"We could be in my room, ordering some food," I say suggestively.

Landon places his fingers on my cheek, caressing it. "We can't skip any steps, Miss Harris. As much as I'd love to drag you back to my room, this is going to go slowly."

"Even if it kills us with desire?"

"Where's your patience?" He kisses the back of my neck. "Imagine how good it'll be when it finally happens... So fucking good." He winks at me.

FOR YEARS, I've had the illusion that skating at Rockefeller center is magical. I blame John Cusack and Kate Beckinsale for letting me believe that the most romantic moment in my life would happen in Manhattan as I hold the hand of the man I love. Even when I spotted a gleam of desire in Landon's mesmerizing blue eyes, the hour at the ice rink wasn't as life changing as I had hoped.

In Kentbury, at night we have the light of the moon to illuminate the lake. We're surrounded by trees, the mountains, and snow.

"Maybe I put too much pressure on the ice rink, and that's why it didn't live up to its expectations," I conclude as we enter the hotel.

Landon's busy with his phone. Maybe he's texting with Cassie or talking to one of his employees. I'm sure he's not paying attention to my rant. I don't blame him. He's not one to watch rom-coms and expect that special moment to happen.

I am a different story. For the past eighteen years, I've been waiting for him to stand at the end of my driveway and serenade me with a boombox like Lloyd did in *Say Anything*. If not that, maybe he can sing "Can't Take My Eyes Off You," like Patrick Verona did in *Ten Things I Hate About You*. I still hold out hope that he might list all the reasons why he loves me when it's New Year's Eve like Harry did with Sally.

"It's a touristy spot, like the artificial pond we have on Main Street," Landon says as we head toward the elevator. "Not everything you watch in movies can live in real life and vice versa." He slumps his shoulders and sighs. "*Serendipity* was actually filmed at Wollman Rink, in Central Park," he says, matter-of-factly.

"And there's that. Though, I guess it's romantic for someone who doesn't have a frozen lake in their backyard," I say.

"There's another selling point. Remind me about it next week, please," he requests. "Isn't the lake part of the vineyard?"

"Technically, but the McCalls always let everyone enjoy it. Are you planning on making it private?" I gLandon at him, tempted to ask him questions about his plans and wanting to give him ideas.

"You'll find out next week," he says. "As I explained earlier, this is a vacation. You're off the clock. When was the last time you even went on vacation?"

I stare at the lights twinkling on the big Christmas tree. It's been years since any of us have gone on a trip that doesn't involve work. The only time my brothers or I leave home is to attend a conference or for training. We love what we do, but we're consumed by work.

"You don't take time off either," I reply casually,

stepping into the elevator and smiling at the couple who joins us.

"When Cassie and I visit Holden, we're on vacation. I check out completely," he says, poking the number to our floor.

"You call me," I argue.

"That's because I need to hear your voice every day," he mumbles. "It's almost impossible for me to exist when you're not around."

He lowers his forehead to mine. My heart kicks against my ribs, and it's not only the fact that he's right in my personal space, but that he's admitting he needs me as much as I do him. I stretch my neck and kiss him lightly. And I hate that we have other people in the elevator, there's no privacy.

As soon as we get closer to our rooms, Landon suggests we go to his room. When we step inside, my mouth opens slightly in awe.

His room is bigger than mine. There's a table for two on the left side next to the balcony. There's a trail of red rose petals leading toward it. Instead of candles, Christmas lights are hanging from the walls. As he closes the door, Van Morrison's "Brown Eyed Girl" begins to play.

Chapter Eighteen

Knightly

"I KNOW it's Peter Gabriel's song that should be playing, but this song reminds me of you," he says, watching me cautiously as if he's waiting for me to move.

Landon looks at me with a predatory gaze I've never seen from him before. The heat in his eyes makes me hotter than the sun on a summer's day. My heartbeat pounds faster and harder as he closes the distance between us.

"You want to eat?" His voice is deep and sexy.

"Is there a second option?" I try to sound suggestive, but my voice comes out like a croak or a gasp, I'm not entirely sure what that sound is, but I clamp my mouth, flustered.

"You're adorable." His eyes shine tenderly. His sexy laugh vibrates through my entire body, and I want to press myself against him and kiss him. I want to feel his beard against my skin.

His hands slide behind my head as he watches me with an intense gaze. His mouth devours mine. The kiss is hungry. It's urgent. The taste of him feeds my own hunger along with his scent and his heat.

"I'll never get enough of you," he says in a husky voice, flicking his tongue against mine.

We embrace as we kiss. His hands on my back. His fingers reaching for the hem of my sweater. I slide my hands under his sweater, moaning as I feel the warmth of his skin, and trace the ripples of his muscles.

He pulls me down to the bed, drawing me over his lap when his phone begins to ring. We ignore it. Breathing and panting, as we keep kissing and touching. Then, my phone starts ringing instead of his. When I recognize Dad's ringtone, I jolt.

"Cassie," I say, peeling myself from his body and taking my phone out of the back pocket of my jeans.

"Hey, Dad," I greet him between pants.

"Are you okay, sweetie?" he asks.

"Yeah, of course," I say, catching my breath. "What's going on?"

"It's Cassie's bedtime, and she hasn't spoken to either one of you," he reminds me. I check the time, and it's fifteen past eight.

"Is she okay?" Landon asks with a thick, rough voice.

"Yes, we forgot to call her," I say, feeling guilty.

He checks his phone and curses under his breath. I tap my phone to switch the call to FaceTime, and the first thing Dad says is, "Why is it so dark?"

My cheeks heat up, and I'm speechless. I might be thirty-two, but I don't want to tell my father what I was about to do.

"You caught us as we were arriving," Landon answers and takes my phone while turning on the lights. "Where's Cassie?"

"Hey, Daddy." Cassie appears on the screen. "I miss you."

"Hi, sweetie," he greets her and his face beams. "How was your day?"

"Is Lee with you?"

I come closer to Landon and greet her. She gives me a big smile, warming up my heart. "Hey, baby girl."

"Did you get me my special present yet?"

"I'll work on it tomorrow," I inform her. "Have you been good to Grandpa?"

She nods firmly.

"Have you helped him with Bob?"

"Yes, and he's been sleeping with me," she says, smiling widely.

We sit by the table, and while we're having dinner, she tells us about her day. Bishop drove her to school on the snowmobile. She helped Bethany with Saturday's wedding since the flower girl isn't arriving until Friday.

"I want to be a flower girl," she requests.

"If either one of your uncles gets married, I'll convince the bride to choose you as one of the flower girls," I offer.

"What about your wedding?"

"Cassie, it's already nine," Landon interrupts. "It's time for bed."

"Don't forget what you promised me, Daddy," she pouts.

After the call, I ask curiously, "What did you promise?"

He sighs. "You."

"What?"

"Hear me out before you walk out on me," he requests, holding my hand. "I already planned to come with you to New York. I had made all the arrangements with your dad and Carson. Later, when I came home, and Cassie was in bed, she said you were leaving and asked me to give you what you wanted so you can be her mom."

My heart pounds harder and harder against my ribcage. Cassie has never asked for her mom or been curious about having a mother. She's content with Landon. It's the two of them.

"Look, I don't want to skip steps and talk about the future when you're still not sure about my feelings. Ideally, one day I'd love to marry you, have kids with you, and if you find it in your heart to adopt Cassie—"

"She's mine," I gasp. "I mean, I know she's not really mine, but I feel as if she's a part of me."

He shakes his head.

"I should've acted sooner," he says, standing up and extending his hand to me.

"It's never too late," I remind him as he wraps his arms around me, resting his interlaced hands on my lower back.

Our heads nod to the rhythm of Van Morrison. My head rests on his torso and I close my eyes briefly, hoping that whatever happens next includes Cassie and Landon.

Chapter Nineteen

Knightly

IT'S BEEN YEARS, almost two whole decades that I've been waiting for Landon to look at me the way he's been doing for the past couple of days. He's familiar. I'm used to having him close. My body is trained to keep itself in check when he's around, even when my heart is pounding like a jackhammer. I should be elated about this next step. I stand frozen as the reality of what's about to happen hits me like a lightning bolt.

Everything between us is about to change.

"Are you okay?" he asks, sliding an arm around my waist, locking me against his hard, powerful body.

I shiver as his fingers trail slowly over my face, tracing the lines of my jaw and the curve of my lips, as if he's studying every inch of me. I don't breathe or speak, afraid that I might wake up from this dream. My eyes flutter shut as his lips brush mine gently. The heat of his body fires up my insides.

"Lee," he says my name in awe. "My sweet Knightly Rose."

He lowers his forehead to mine; I open my eyes, and our gazes connect. "You're one of the most important people in my world—my life. This, our relationship, matters a lot to me. I'm risking it because I love you."

"You do?" I ask. I'm shaking under his grasp as I wait for his next move. "It's too soon, I mean we just started to date—"

"I worked hard to fight my attraction to you." His eyes move toward my mouth and then back to my eyes. "To bury my feelings for you. God knows it's been getting harder as time passes. At night, I've imagined having mind-blowing sex with you. Thought about peeling off every piece of clothing you wear until there's not one barrier between my mouth and your soft skin."

His mouth is so close to mine that I can feel how intoxicating the warmth of his breath is. I hold my breath waiting for him to kiss me again with the sensual hunger he's been kissing me with for the past couple of days. Instead, his lips slide over my jaw, down to the back of my ear. My breathing becomes erratic as his tongue traces a line to my neck. Everything inside me melts. I hold on to his shoulders as he nibbles the sensitive skin at the base of my throat.

Mouth exploring, hands moving down my body, and the intense gaze undressing me is pushing me to the edge, but not soon enough.

He's taking his time, and I'm impatient for more. His hands, his mouth, his scent, and the feel of him. Every cell of my body shakes, waiting for more. I just can't leave it to him. I tug his long sleeve shirt off, exposing his muscular chest. I press my hands over his shoulders, running them down his powerful body. Feeling each ripple, swell, and dip of his muscles.

Feeling bold, I snap open the button of his jeans and slowly pull down the zipper. I lick my lips when I realize he's not wearing any underwear and dare to close my hand over his thick length.

"Lee." He shudders as I pump him a couple of times. "Please, don't," he groans, pulling me into a deep, hungry kiss.

He thrusts his tongue inside my mouth, exploring every inch of it. I match his speed and demand more from him.

Without saying a word or moving too much, he pulls off my sweater and the turtleneck I'm wearing underneath. Then, he runs his hands down my body, peeling off my jeans, and leaving me in the cute set of black lace I bought yesterday especially for him to see. He presses his mouth between my breasts. Licks one nipple, and then the other, wetting the lacy bra. My nipples are hard like pearls. They're swollen, waiting to be freed and sucked by him.

He stops and grabs my face gently between both of his hands. "I want you so much, are you sure about this?"

"I want you too," I say and gasp as he lifts me and sets me on the bed.

Landon moves his hand slowly, traveling from my heel, passing through the inside of my thigh, and stopping right at my core. He runs a finger over the wet fabric of my panties and draws a few circles around it with his thumb. I moan.

"You're torturing me, Miller," I complain as he slides one finger through the thin fabric and touches my clit.

"I'm enjoying you before I feast," he says, claiming my mouth.

As he kisses me, his hand slides down my back, unhooking my bra and releasing my breasts. He continues tracing my skin until his fingers meet my hips, and he pushes the lacy fabric all the way down, leaving me completely naked and at his mercy. His mouth follows, stopping to suck my nipples, alternating them as his fingers stroke, explore, and rub my heat.

I grab onto the sheets as a million sensations cascade

from everywhere. My breathing is too fast, I can't focus on anything, and all I can smell is his woodsy aftershave. I feel as if can't take any more but at the same time I want him to continue.

His lips move away and I whimper, but gasp as his hands part my labia and he sucks me. His tongue laps me, while he thrusts a finger inside my channel and pumps it fast. My body begins to tremble as he pushes me right to the edge, and I soar. I'm at the highest peak of a mountain, spent but needy.

He stands up, reaching for the condom he placed on the nightstand. His eyes are on fire, glowing like a torch illuminating the end of a tunnel. He rolls on the condom, but his eyes barely leave my body.

"Are you ready?" he asks with a soft voice, his blue gaze never releasing me.

"I've never been more sure of anything."

Slowly, he lowers himself down. The head of his cock right at my entrance. Our mouths crash against each other as he fills me slowly with his thickness. He's careful as he gives me time to adjust to his length.

I close my eyes for a couple of beats and when I open them, he's watching me. "Breathe, baby, you're safe with me."

I gasp, taking some air before he pulls his shaft out and thrusts back in. This time he doesn't wait for me to adjust. He starts rocking against me faster, moving with urgency. But it's not hard, at least, not as hard as I believe he could be doing it. He's gentle, the way he's always been with me. Gentle and loving.

"You're the most beautiful woman in the world," he mumbles against my mouth.

"I love you," I mutter, clinging onto his shoulders. "I love you so much, Landon."

He pumps inside me, deeper and harder. We're becoming an extension of each other. He doesn't hold back anymore. His movements are raw, primal. We lose control. Our breathing is erratic. Our bodies meld together just as our hearts and our souls become one.

I twist and thrash as my muscles convulse and he's right behind me, shaking on top of me. He groans and thrusts himself even deeper, making me come even harder. We are flying high, skyrocketing to the ultimate place.

Landon drops his head on my shoulder, gasping for air just like I am.

"I love you, Lee," he murmurs, almost spent, and rolls me around, keeping me in a tight embrace. "I'm all yours. I gave you my heart, now my body, and you own my soul."

As he cradles me in his arms, we look into each other's eyes and smile. He kisses my shoulder and rolls over to the other side of the bed, reaching toward the nightstand.

"Knightly Rose. Lee," he says, rising from the bed and bending down on one knee.

He stares at me, holding a red box that contains a gorgeous diamond solitaire ring.

"Landon," I gasp.

"I love that you eat ice cream even when it's minus twenty degrees outside. I love that you always look after everyone. I love that you welcomed my daughter and loved her as if she were yours. I've loved you in many different ways since we were kids. My love for you has evolved as we've grown older. I came to New York to convince you that you're the love of my life. I'm not perfect, but you make me perfect."

He clears his throat. "Lee, will you marry me?"

"Yes." I look into his clear blue eyes before I throw myself into his arms. "Of course I will."

Epilogue

Landon

It's Christmas day. Like every year, we're at Grandpa Harris's house, having brunch and opening presents. I look outside the big window, staring at the snow-dusted forest, ice crystals shimmering on the surface of the lake. It's a perfect white Christmas. Cassie is right by the tree, unwrapping boxes and squealing with happiness. Lee's right beside her, snapping pictures of our daughter. Until her gaze meets mine.

As usual, she doesn't need to speak for me to know

what she needs. I walk to her, extend my hand and help her stand. I wrap my arms around her, enjoying the feel of her body against mine, kissing the top of her head.

"She's happy," Lee whispers.

"Are you happy?" I ask.

"Mom, can we make cookies?" Cassie questions, showing her the cookie cutters Santa brought her.

Lee's chin quivers. Her eyes fill with moisture. "Yes," she answers with a quiet voice.

"It's okay if I call you Mom, right?"

Lee moves from my grasp and opens her arms for Cassie. "Of course, it is, sweetheart. I love you so much."

"I love you too, Mom," Cassie says before jetting off to the kitchen.

I smile at Lee and kiss her nose.

I never thought I could possibly love her more, but I was wrong. Every day I fall more and more in love with her. I adore this woman with all my heart. The woman who loves me for who I am. Our lives are perfect for us.

We're getting married next year. The McCalls accepted my offer. We'll take possession of the vineyard in early January. Lee and I plan on building a house right by the lake, big enough to fit our family. For now, Cassie and I are moving into Lee's house.

"Yes, I'm happy," Lee finally answers, wrapping her arms around my neck. "You and Cassie make my life magical, perfect."

. . .

Do you want more Kentbury?

Everything is falling apart.

I just got fired—by my father.

My boyfriend decided I wasn't good enough—during my Grandma's funeral.

That hot guy I met at the bar—I didn't get one kiss from him.

All I have left is to start a new life.

But before I embark into the unknown, I head to Kentbury.

Someone has to warn my paternal grandmother that her son wants to leave her destitute.

And who do I find instead?

Tall, hot, and delicious Bishop Harris.

My failed one-night stand.

He's trying to run me out of town.

But between the autumn festivals, apple picking, and hard cider, things get a lot more interesting

I go from trying to avoid the small town to wondering if I can spend more than Fall in Kentbury.

Read Bishop's book >>>> Fall in Kentbury

Dear Reader

Dear Reader,

Happy Holidays!

Thank you so much for taking time out of your life to read Christmas in Kentbury. I had lots of fun asking my reading group what they'd like to see in a holiday book. They chose a single dad, friends-to-lovers romance. I hope you fall in love with Landon and all the characters as much as I did.

Are we going to revisit Kentbury? I hope so. I fell in love with the town, the Harrises and also the Millers. Mrs. Bowman knows so much about the town. I'm not sure when this will happen but maybe early next fall you might be able to visit them again.

After you're done reading, I'd appreciate if you leave a review on Amazon, Barnes & Noble, Goodreads, or

Bookbub. And if possible, spread the love around by sharing.

Subscribe to my newsletter to find out about upcoming releases, extra scenes, and special offers.

Sending you hugs and all my love,

Claudia

What to read after CiK?

If you love single dad romances, I have a few more recommendations:
  My One Regret
  As We Are
  Finally Found You

Best friends to Lovers
  Suddenly Broken
  Call You Mine
  Perfect for Me

Small Town
  Loved You Once
  Finally You

Faking the Game

You can check my entire back list at the end of the book.

Fall in Kentbury

McKay

"Here's to the shittiest week of *your life*." Lou, my older sister, raises her margarita glass, the corners of her mouth turning up in a wry smile.

The low hum of laughter and clinking glasses surrounds us as we sit in a crowded bar. I'm not sure coming here tonight was such a good idea, but I didn't have much else to do. I force my lips into a tight smile and lightly clink my glass against hers. "And just as the holidays are coming up. Joy," I add flatly.

There won't be couple Halloween costumes, Thanksgiving with the family, nor a white Christmas tucked in Switzerland. Okay, the last one was my idea—a way to avoid my parents—but I hoped my boyfriend would agree.

Honestly, I should be at home right now, hidden away in the darkest corner of my bedroom, a tub of ice cream my only companion as tears flow freely while I grieve for the grandmother I barely knew. Plus, mending a broken heart. But I'm not filled with grief since my mother didn't nurture my relationship with Grandma Pili. And there's certainly not sadness that Reginald Maloni Olsen the Fourth so abruptly ended our relationship.

Though, I'm pissed he did it during my grandmother's funeral.

"So, are you ready for a trip down to see Grandma Eugenia?" Lou asks, ice cubes tinkling against her margarita glass. Her eyes flash with curiosity as she takes a sip.

"This is completely unfair. Why is it that I, the youngest, have been chosen for this honor?" My words drip with disbelief and irritation. Five siblings, yet the shitty jobs always fall on me.

Lou shrugs. "Simple hierarchy, my little one. Plus, it's not like you have anything to do."

The last comment feels like a jab to the throat. Seriously, did she have to go there?

"It's not my fault that my job went poof." I make a gesture with my hands, as if I just performed a magic trick and made something disappear into thin air. "Gone forever."

My gaze drifts to my empty glass. I point at it, silently requesting a refill from the bartender. Of everything that's been happening in my life lately, losing my job cut me the deepest. It wasn't my dream job, but I'd worked for my father since my junior year of college.

I spent nine years of my life trying to show him I could be an asset. But the moment his bottom line teetered on the brink of red, what did he do? He eliminated positions and fired about a thousand employees—including his youngest daughter—me.

A bitter laugh escapes me. "Who knew saving a sinking ship meant throwing your own daughter overboard?"

The bartender refills my glass. I lift it and swirl it a couple times, staring into its amber depths, hoping to drown my anger, so I can continue doing my parents' bidding without snapping.

If Dad had listened to little McKay, his company wouldn't be in trouble. But I'm not one of his sons. My parents cling to archaic norms where a woman's only worth lies in marriage and motherhood—in other words, they're misogynistic assholes.

Obviously, my parents and I don't see eye to eye. Ever since I can remember, I've been the misfit. Soon, Mom will start parading eligible suitors before me, prized stallions vying to replace my ex. Ideally, some heir with old money, a spotless reputation, and bulging accounts—the perfect match in their eyes. I smirk cynically. As if that would ever make me happy. I wish they could understand my aspirations are not theirs.

In fact, I wish I had aspirations of my own. I've been so wrapped up in meeting their needs, trying to make them proud, that I don't even know what I want to do with my life. This Vermont trip suddenly doesn't seem like such a bad idea. It can be an escape from my parents' rehearsed lectures and expectations.

As for my job situation, obviously I want to work, but what am I supposed to do now? I'm no longer the SEO for one of the top 500 companies. Honestly, I don't want to continue doing the same thing anyway.

The possibilities of a new future brighten my mood. I picture the peaceful Vermont countryside. Well, I've never actually been there, but I'm sure it's just like in those Hallmark movies—trees, snow, and hot cocoa around every corner. I wish Father had taken us to visit my grandparents growing up. But he doesn't have much contact with anyone in his family. As far as I know, he just calls his mother once a year and has his assistant send presents for the holidays.

I'm pretty sure my father loves just three things: my

mother, money, and … well, I hope us children too. His disdain for his own mother makes me wonder if she's as cold as he is. Will she even care to leave her small town to be closer to her son?

He wants Grandma to sell all her properties to a friend, so he can use the money to save his company. The corner of my lip lifts as I wonder what would happen if, instead of being my parents' puppet, I warn Grandma about their motives.

"Whatever you're thinking, don't," Lou warns, narrowing her gaze at me.

I bat my eyelashes innocently. "Excuse me?"

"I know that smirk," she says. "Just remember, if you don't go to Vermont, they'll send me instead. And I'm not leaving my children at the mercy of our crazy mother while my husband is working."

Lou's phone pings mid-rant, lighting up her face with a radiant smile. "It's Tony," she exclaims, voice brimming with so much joy you'd think they just started dating.

Seeing her excitement stirs an ache inside me. Will I ever find someone who loves me like Tony loves her? They've been together since college but still act like besotted newlyweds. I watch as Lou giggles looking at her phone, eyes sparkling as she texts with her other half. I can't help but envy their relationship.

"Off to your husband and children," I quip playfully, waving a hand dismissively.

Lou shakes her head, brow furrowed in concern. "You need me."

"That's nonsense." I cross my heart like I used to when I was a child and she was babysitting. "I promise to be on my best behavior. You don't have to worry about me." I shrug with feigned nonchaLandon, masking what could be my best move yet.

"But you were dumped, and now you're unemployed," Lou says, squeezing my hand, eyes searching mine.

"I'm fine," I assure her. "It's not like life has ended. If anything, I don't have to deal with Reginald and the crappiest sex of my life anymore." I take a long sip, finishing my drink. "I might find someone who's actually good in bed and can give me an orgasm. Or two."

Lou cringes, leaning in to hiss, "Use your indoor voice, please," under her breath.

I erupt in uncontrolled laughter, the sound bubbling out. Okay, I might be a little tipsy and should restrain myself. But instead, I impulsively gulp Lou's drink in one swallow.

No one can blame me for drinking myself stupid. I have a lot to think about this weekend, and I just don't have the bandwidth for any of it. I'm twenty-nine without a clear direction on what I want to do with my life, and a family that's too self-involved to even see that I'm a little lost. I know Lou is trying to help, but she's more likely just trying to make sure I don't shirk my duties and leave everything to her.

A reckless idea occurs to me: what if, instead of going to Vermont to convince my estranged grandmother to leave, I'm the one who disappears?

I could sell my condo and leave Boston, sever all ties. Become someone new out west. McKay Margaret McFolley could vanish into anonymity.

Lou gently shakes her head, wordlessly disapproving as the bartender closes our tab with her credit card. "Don't tempt fate," she orders sternly. "Go home."

A sigh spills from my lips. "Alright, fine, I won't do anything crazy," I concede, a small grin tugging at the corners of my mouth.

Lou responds with an exaggerated eye roll, knowing her little sister might do something reckless. She slips away, rushing through the busy tables and out of the bar.

Alone now, I turn to the bartender. "You know what I need?"

He quirks an eyebrow.

"To get laid." The words leave me recklessly before I clap a hand over my mouth, eyes wide. Seriously, what is wrong with me tonight? I should go home and sober up before I do something stupid.

As if summoned, a man slides onto the stool beside me. "Well, hello there," he says, his voice low and gravelly.

I'm momentarily stunned by his rugged handsomeness—sun-kissed hair. He's casual yet sexy. His brown eyes meet mine, sparking a jittery feeling in my stomach. A subtle smile teases at his lips, sending my pulse racing. Tall and muscular with broad shoulders and biceps straining against his shirtsleeves. His self-assured stance radiates a quiet strength that makes my knees weak.

The smirk, though … that smirk seems to promise something more. Maybe this will be the rebellious thing I'll do instead of telling my grandmother to ignore her son. But can I jump into bed with a stranger?

One reckless night to break free from expectations? Or will I listen to my doubts and go home alone?

Claudia is an award-winning, *USA Today* bestselling author.

She writes alluring, thrilling stories about complicated women and the men who take their breaths away. Her books are the perfect blend of steamy and heartfelt, filled with emotional characters and explosive chemistry. Her writing takes readers to new heights, providing a variety of tears, laughs, and shocking moments that leave fans on the edge of their seats.

She lives in Denver, Colorado with her husband, her youngest two children, and three fluffy dogs.

When Claudia is not writing, you can find her reading, knitting, or just hanging out with her family. At nights, she likes to binge watches shows or movies with her equally geeky husband.

To find more about Claudia:
  website

Be sure to sign up for my newsletter where you'll receive news about upcoming releases, sneak previous, and also FREE books from other bestselling authors.

Also By Claudia Burgoa

Be sure to sign up for my newsletter where you'll receive news about upcoming releases, sneak previous, and also FREE books from other bestselling authors.

Christmas in Kentbury is also available in Audio

The Baker's Creek Billionaire Brothers Series

Loved You Once

A Moment Like You

Defying Our Forever

Call You Mine

As We Are

Yours to Keep

Collide with Me

Paradise Bay Billionaire Brothers

My Favorite Night

Faking The Game

Can't Help Love

Along Came You

My Favorite Mistake

The Way of Us

Meant For Me

Finally Found You

Where We Belong

Heartwood Lake Secret Billionaires

A Place Like You

Dirty Secret Love

Love Unlike Ours

Through It All

Better than Revenge

Fade into us

An Unlikely Story

Hard to love

Against All Odds Series

Wrong Text, Right Love

Didn't Expect You

Love Like Her

Until Next Time, Love

Something Like Love

Accidentally in Love

Decker Family Novels

Fall for Me

Fight for Me

Perfect for Me

Forever with Me

Kentbury Tales

Christmas in Kentbury

Fall in Kentbury

Standalones

Chasing Fireflies

Until I Fall

Finding My Reason

Something Like Hate

Someday, Somehow

Chaotic Love Duet

Begin with You

Back to You

Co-writing

Holiday with You

Home with You

Here with You

All my books are interconnected standalone, except for the duets, but if you want a reading order, I have it here ↬ Reading Order

Made in the USA
Columbia, SC
07 October 2024

43211129R00114